Cumbria Library Services

County Council

This book is due for return on or before the last date above.
It may be renewed by personal application, post or telephone,
if not in demand.

C.L. 18F

*Indulge in some perfect romance
from the incomparable*

PENNY JORDAN

**The all new Penny Jordan
large print collection gives you
your favourite glamorous
Penny Jordan stories in
easier-to-read print.**

Penny Jordan has been writing for more than twenty-five years and has an outstanding record: over 165 novels published including the phenomenally successful A PERFECT FAMILY, TO LOVE, HONOUR AND BETRAY, THE PERFECT SINNER and POWER PLAY which hit *The Sunday Times* and *New York Times* bestseller lists. She says she hopes to go on writing until she has passed the 200 mark, and maybe even the 250 mark.

Penny is a member and supporter of both the Romantic Novelists' Association and the Romance Writers of America—two organisations dedicated to providing support for both published and yet-to-be published authors.

CAPTIVE
AT THE SICILIAN
BILLIONAIRE'S
COMMAND

Penny Jordan

First published in Great Britain 2009
by Mills & Boon, an imprint of Harlequin (UK) Limited.
Large Print edition 2011
Harlequin (UK) Limited,
Eton House, 18-24 Paradise Road,
Richmond, Surrey TW9 1SR

© Penny Jordan 2009

ISBN: 978 0 263 22955 4

Harlequin (UK) policy is to use papers that are natural,
renewable and recyclable products and made from
wood grown in sustainable forests. The logging and
manufacturing process conform to the legal environmental
regulations of the country of origin.

Printed and bound in Great Britain
by CPI Antony Rowe, Chippenham, Wiltshire

PROLOGUE

ROCCO threw down the hard hat he had been wearing whilst he showed the 'suits' and potential investors round the new complex—a luxury spa and holiday resort here on Sicily—pushing an impatient hand into the thick darkness of his hair as he held the mobile to his ear and said laconically, 'You wanted me, Don Falcon?'

If his elder brother was irritated by Rocco's mocking use of his title he didn't say so, announcing coolly instead, 'We've found her. Here is her address in London. You know what you have to do.'

Falcon had ended the call before Rocco could say anything, leaving him to retrieve his hard hat and stride towards the Porta cabin that was currently serving as his on-site office.

CHAPTER ONE

A LOUD bang from a noisy exhaust somewhere in the street had Julie glancing over her shoulder and then checking automatically to see that her shabby shoulder bag was tucked in against her body. This was a down-at-heel and often unsafe neighbourhood. Only the other day she had been warned by the woman in charge of the nursery never to leave any personal documents in her flat as there had been a spate of robberies, with passports especially being targeted. As a result, she was now carrying their passports with her in her handbag.

'Ms Simmonds?'

Julie gasped with shock. She had been so busy looking over her shoulder that she hadn't seen the man who was now standing in front of her, blocking her way to the entrance of the converted house where she rented a small flat.

One look at him, though, told her that this was no thief. Not with that expensive car parked right next to them, which she hadn't noticed before and which she suspected must be his.

Warily she nodded her head.

'And this is *your* child?'

Now she could feel herself tensing, hesitating, as she held on tightly to her orphaned baby nephew whilst she fought off her feeling of apprehension. Josh *was* her child after all—now. The icy March rain that had started when she had left the local eight-until-ten shop where she worked part-time to walk to the nursery to collect Josh had soaked through her thin coat, turning the fine silver-blonde silkiness of her hair into lank rats' tails whilst the cold had left her skin blue-white and bloodless, and now she was trapped here on the street with a man who was asking her questions she did not want to answer. The weight of Josh, plus his nappy bag and her handbag, were already making her thin arms ache.

'If you're a debt collector…' she began. Her voice might be thin with disdain and exhaustion, but it was fear that was making her heart thud so painfully. Josh *was* hers. There was no reason for

her to feel that this man—this stranger—
somehow threatened her right to call Josh her
child, even if she wasn't actually Josh's birth
mother. That was what living a hand-to-mouth
existence and constantly fearing the arrival of
another demand for money did for you: it made
you feel guilty and on edge even when you had
no cause to do so.

If it *was* money that this man was after then he
was wasting his time. Julie's chin unconsciously
lifted with the pride she knew he would believe
she no longer had the right to have. There was no
point in anyone sending in any more bailiffs as
there was nothing left to take. Even Josh's buggy
had been claimed against her dead sister's debts.
There was no point feeling sorry for herself or
wishing that her parents had thought to make a
proper will. Ultimately, as their now only surviv-
ing child, she should inherit something—
enough, she hoped, to clear all Judy's debts and
buy a small house for herself and Josh. But according to her solicitor a final settlement of everything could be some time away, given the
complications of the situation.

The fact was that her parents, her sister,

James—her sister's fiancé—and his parents had all died, along with twenty other people in the same fatal train crash. It had been such a terrible shock, and had left Julie with the task of supporting herself and her late sister's child whilst being hounded to pay Judy's debts. And, of course, cope with James's death.

The funerals had been in their way even worse than the news of the deaths itself. She, of course, as the only adult living member of her own family, had had to make the arrangements for the burial of her parents and her sister. She had thought that maybe Judy should be buried with James, but Annette, James's elder sister and only relative, had refused to entertain the idea, insisting that James was buried with their parents.

With the funeral two days after her family's, Julie had been able to attend—and she had found that Annette was exactly as James had once described his elder sister to her. Polished and expensively dressed—her husband was a banker—and very cold.

'Keep that child away from me,' she had said sharply, stepping back from Julie. 'My coat cost a fortune, it's pure cashmere.'

James had told Julie that Roger, Annette's husband, desperately wanted a family but that Annette flatly refused to entertain the idea. They had a smart townhouse in Chelsea, where Annette entertained Roger's colleagues and clients. She was very much the corporate wife, and according to James was very ambitious for her husband. James. Julie blinked away exhausted tears. Her one and only love. Her one and only lover. It only things had been different. If only *she* had been the one to conceive his child. If only…

Losing him still hurt so very much. Only with his death had she admitted that somewhere deep inside herself she had been cherishing the foolish hope that one day he would come back to her.

Rocco watched the shadows come and go in the woman's unusually expressive dark grey eyes. The only part of her that looked anything like alive. He had never seen such a washed-out-looking female.

'A debt collector?' He gave her a haughty look, before adding dryly, 'You could call me that,' he agreed, answering Julie's bitter question.

'Although what I'm here for is more properly a matter of repossession.'

Repossession? There wasn't anything left in the flat to repossess. The bailiffs had taken it all. She tried to look braver than she felt as she looked at the man.

The harsh street lighting gave his features a Byzantine quality of polished arrogance allied to cruelty, gilding the olive skin drawn tight over the high cheekbones. It was the face of a man without mercy or compassion—the face of a man whose heritage was rooted in the alien and the dangerous, Julie recognised.

It was hard for Rocco to see what could possibly have attracted his young half-brother to this pale plain English girl. She was thin to the point of malnourishment, whey-faced, and so far as he could see without charm or personality— but perhaps he was being unfair. Given enough champagne and the illegal party drugs his late half-brother had favoured, maybe she had sparkled in the tawdry manner in which Antonio had liked his women to sparkle.

Distaste filled him—for his late half-brother's way of life, for the morals of the woman standing in front of him, but most of all for the duty that had been imposed upon him by his own birth and his elder brother's conscience.

He had been against this whole thing right from the start. A child's place was with its mother. But Alessandro had pointed out that the child *would* be with its mother, at all times, and would continue to remain with her since Rocco's task was to bring them both back to Sicily with him. In fact, now that he had seen the circumstances in which the pair of them seemed to be living, Rocco acknowledged that his intervention in their lives could only be of benefit—to them both.

She was so cold, and she must get Josh inside—but *he* was still standing in front her. Josh still wasn't over the nasty cough he had caught at the beginning of the winter.

Poor baby, he had had so many problems since her sister had given birth to him three weeks early, in January. First there had been the fact that Judy had never wanted him in the first place. Then there had been his inability to feed properly, followed by the discovery that he was slightly tongue-tied… That had led to a very minor medical procedure, after which—perhaps because Judy had not been careful enough—he had contracted an infection, which in turn had led to further feeding problems. And then with one blow fate had robbed him of his parents and both sets of grandparents.

But somehow Julie would make it up to him. She would love him and look after him. He was, after all, all she had left of James and her family, even if he hadn't already been precious to her in his own right.

When they had come to tell her about the train accident which had killed so many people, including her own and Josh's family, she had made a silent vow to the man she loved so much to love and protect the child he had believed was his.

James had been so proud and excited when he had discovered that Judy was pregnant…

Rocco was getting impatient. He was a Leopardi after all. The Leopardis had ruled their lands and dispensed their own form of law in Sicily from the time of the Crusades onwards. Rocco had grown up in an environment where to be a Leopardi meant that one's word was law.

'I don't know what it is you wish to repossess,' Julie began tiredly, 'but my…my baby is cold, and I really need to get him inside.' She didn't really want to have to open her handbag in front of this stranger, but she needed to get her keys so that she could let herself into the flat. It wasn't easy, trying to surreptitiously open her handbag and at the same time hold Josh safe, and when she saw the way the man was looking at her, with a mix of male irritation and impatience, she knew that her attempt at discretion had been a waste of time.

'Let me hold the child for you.' The cool assurance in the male voice combined with the unexpected offer caused Julie's eyes to widen in astonishment. He sounded as though he was perfectly at home holding young babies.

'You've got children of your own?' Julie's face burned as she realised how personal and inappropriate her question was.

His terse 'No' compounded those feelings, which hardly inspired her to hand over Josh. But then her ineffectual scrabbling one-handedly in the bag suddenly caused it to tilt upwards, disgorging some of its contents onto the wet street, including her purse, an assortment of bills that

belonged to Judy, her keys and their passports—
Josh's a sad reminder of the honeymoon her
sister had been so excited about, their first
holiday as a family. Rocco frowned as he looked
down at the wet pavement and saw the passports
amongst the other detritus that had spilled from
the woman's handbag.

Ignoring Julie's gasp of protest, he bent down
to retrieve her possessions, picking up the now
wet bills and the two passports before casually
flicking them open. Both passports were in his
hand—a providential accident or a potent sign
that this task might after all be simpler and easier
than he had thought? What kind of woman
carried passports around with her? he wondered,
and then grimaced as he found the answer to his
own question.

Obviously the kind who expected that the opportunity to leave the country might occur at any time
and wanted to be prepared for it. He imagined it
was the kind of thing that would be quite common
where high-class hookers were concerned.

But this pathetic and unappealing-looking
woman couldn't have looked less like anything
high-class. Rocco reached for her purse,

frowning as he felt its emptiness, and then picked up her keys.

He was handing everything back to her, including her keys. Julie exhaled shakily in relief. She wasn't sure just what she had been fearing, but now she admitted she did feel a bit more relaxed—or at least she did until he said autocractically, 'The baby needs to be out of this rain and wind.' He put his hand on her arm, nodding in the direction of his car as he told her, 'My car's over there.'

Had she moved of her own volition, or was it a combination of the wind and his hand on her arm that had somehow brought her so close to his car that she was standing with it on one side of her and him on the other, hemming her in? Julie shivered.

What were his intentions? What did he really want? Not her. Not a man like this one, whose every movement and expression suggested a certain contempt for everything and anything that was not of the very best—including the speed with which his hand had dropped from her arm. All she needed to do was simply ask him to move. She could even push past him. Her hand was beginning to feel numb from clinging on to her possessions, and Josh was an increasingly heavy weight on her arm, despite his slightness. Carefully she tried to adjust Josh's position to ease her arm.

'Let me take him.' He was reaching for Josh, Julie recognised immediately, all maternal anxiety, his hands long-fingered, lean and tanned against the baby's shabby suit.

'What is it you want?' she demanded. 'Who sent you here?'

'No one sends me anywhere,' he told her coldly. 'And it isn't *who* I am from you should be asking, but where.'

'Where? I don't understand what you're talking about.'

'No? Try this, then. I'm from the country and the family to whom the boy belongs.'

Julie's eyes were as grey and drained of warm blue as London's March sky, and they registered shock and then fear as the meaning of his words slammed into her heart, causing it to thud so heavily that she could hear its beat in her own ears.

'You're from Sicily?' she guessed.

'I'm from Sicily,' he agreed.

Of all the possibilities she might have envisaged, this had not even come close to being one of them—and that alone was enough to fling her headlong into mindless panic as she demanded, 'Who are you?'

Rocco wasn't used to having his identity questioned. He looked down at her contemptuously from his six-foot-three height, folding his arms across his chest. The fine wool of his handmade Italian suit moved with him as easily as though it was his flesh.

'My name is Leopardi—Rocco Leopardi. And now that I have answered you perhaps you will be good enough to give me the child—my nephew—and get into the car?'

His *nephew*. So this was not Antonio—the rich, louche Sicilian playboy with whom her sister had had an affair in the South of France early last May, which may or may not have been responsible for Josh's conception—a fact which she had forced Julie to promise to keep a secret from James. A feeling akin to relief which there was absolutely no justification for her to feel warmed the icy sting of Julie's rain-chilled body, temporarily making her drop her guard and momentarily relax her tightly protective hold on the sleeping baby.

Fearing that she was about to drop the child, Rocco immediately reached for him, lifting him bodily out of Julie's arms before she could stop him and then opening the rear passenger door to the car.

'What are you doing?'

Fresh panic and fear filled Julie as she watched Rocco place Josh into a baby seat in the back of the car. Everything about the way he handled her nephew was gentle and protective of the small, vulnerable life, but for some reason the fact that he was being so careful, so caring, actually increased Julie's fear. For herself and her own position in Josh's life?

'I'm simply putting the baby out of harm's way whilst we talk. You almost dropped him.'

'No, that's not true,' Julie denied. 'You're trying to take him away from me, aren't you?' she guessed. 'You're trying to steal him.'

Rocco gave her a tight-lipped look. He might have known she'd be the high-drama hysterical type.

Fear and panic had seized Julie. Did he know that she wasn't really Josh's mother? Was he going to try and claim that she had no rights where Josh was concerned? He was the kind of man from the kind of family who would stop at nothing to get what they wanted, and if they wanted her nephew… Julie's heart was thumping frantically. She could see a man and a woman coming towards them on the opposite side of the road. She opened her mouth to call out to them for help, her instinctive need to protect her relationship with Josh overwhelming her normal dislike of any kind of scene.

'Look—' Rocco had begun intending to point out that she was overreacting, only to stop when he saw that Julie was looking across the road at a couple who were walking towards them. Instantly guessing what she was going to do, he reacted immediately. She was already standing close to the car, so it was easy to hold her there in his arms, and easier still to silence her planned cry for help with the pressure of his mouth on hers.

Normally the last thing he'd have contemplated doing was kissing a woman like this one. She appealed to him almost as little physically as she repulsed him morally—thin, blonde, pale-skinned, and ready to have sex with any man who asked her just so long as he was rich.

Rocco liked strikingly attractive, intelligent women, who showed their pride in themselves in everything they did and were. His father might be the head of one of Sicily's oldest aristocratic families, and he himself might have a courtesy title, but Rocco was a billionaire in his own right, through his own endeavours, and he took pride in that achievement. When the time eventually came that he was ready to settle down—which most definitely was not yet—he wanted a partner who was exactly that: a woman who was equal to truly being his partner. Someone who understood the demands that came with his birthright but who at the same time had made her own way in the world and knew the value of having done so—a woman who was equally at home in society as she was in the corporate world; a woman who held herself aloof from the cheap sexual thrills beloved of his half-brother and his cronies, and who disdained them and everything they represented as much as he did himself; but at the same time a woman who understood and shared his own deep-rooted core sensuality.

One thing she must not do, though, was fall in love with him or expect him to fall in love with her. Bitterness gripped its ever-ready fist tight on his emotions. His mother had loved his father and that love had destroyed her. That was never going to happen to him, nor did he want to be responsible for the pain of it in someone else. He had no intention of becoming either the victim his mother had been or the callous enforcer of that victimisation that was his father.

The child's mother had stiffened in his hold, and he could feel the frightened race of her heartbeat.

Frightened? Of what? Not him? Rocco was outraged. The thought of creating fear within anyone, but especially in someone weaker and vulnerable, was totally abhorrent to him. How could a woman who had given herself to his depraved late half-brother possibly be afraid of him? From what he knew of Antonio, a woman who was frightened of a man's touch was hardly his style. And from what Falcon's sources had discovered about her, this one had been very much Antonio's style—a so-called glamour model. Not that there was anything remotely glamorous about her now…

And yet somehow her lips were unexpectedly soft and full, and her slenderness within his arms disarmed and distracted him, making him want to hold her close, tempting his tongue-tip to explore the shape and tease apart that closed line of denial.

Rocco wasn't used to women who denied him. The reason why Julie had ended up in Rocco's arms had become buried beneath a surge of other feelings and a very different kind of panic. James was the only man she had ever wanted to hold her like this and kiss her like this, Julie thought painfully, but somehow—either through exhaustion or fear or both—she could feel her will to resist him giving way to the warmth emanating from him. It was as though her weakness was irresistibly drawn to his strength, her woman to his man, the softness of her lips to the hard command of his mouth, until the determined male pressure of his tongue was melting her resistance as easily as the heat of a Sicilian summer sun could melt winter snow. Her starving senses were betrayingly greedy for the sensual pleasure of his kiss.

This was how she had once dreamed of James holding her and kissing her—before they had become lovers, before she had lost him to Judy.

It had been bad enough having to listen to James telling her gently that, whilst he liked her and valued their time together, he had fallen in love with Judy, but it had been even worse having to listen to Judy confessing in a drunken moment that she was not sure who was the father of the unwanted child she had been carrying.

It could, she had admitted, be the wealthy Sicilian playboy with whom she'd had an affair but who had since ditched her and was refusing to answer her letters. But she was going to tell James that it was his—because, as she had told Julie smugly and with open malice, it actually could be, seeing as James had rushed her into bed the minute she had returned from Sicily.

Having to listen to Judy telling her about them making love had been pure torture. Julie clung fiercely to Rocco. It had been *her* kisses she had wanted James to long for, her touch, her body… Lost in her own emotions, she felt the man holding her become James, and the intensity of her emotions dictated her actions, so that she was kissing him with all the fierce longing and pride of her love for James.

Julie's sudden passion caught Rocco off guard.

She was pressing her body into his, opening her mouth beneath his, and her breathing was altering to become as unsteady as her heartbeat.

Unaware of the reason for it, instinctively he responded to it, shaping her body to his own, taking the sweetness her parted lips were offering, and letting the soft moan of assent she gave at the first thrust of his tongue be the signal that brought his hands sweeping down her body to bring her intimately close to his own flesh.

The sensation of hard male thighs pressing against her jolted Julie back to reality.

This man was not James.

As soon as he felt her struggle Rocco stopped kissing her, sliding his hands back up over her body more out of habit than desire, as distaste for his own actions filled him. Since when had he ever wanted Antonio's leavings?

It was unthinkable that he should want a woman like this one—a pathetic excuse for a real woman.

He had stopped kissing her, but he was still holding on to her, Julie recognized, shivering in his hold. Why had she kissed him like that? He wasn't anything like James. The couple she would have called out to for help had now, of course, gone.

As much as he wanted to turn his back and walk away from her, and from his own momentary betrayal of himself and his values, Rocco knew that he could not do so. On this occasion his duty to his family must come before any duty to himself.

'There are matters we need to discuss,' he told Julie coldly.

'I will not let you take my baby away from me,' Julie warned him fiercely, blinking back the tears caused by the overload on her emotions.

Rocco frowned at her.

'You are being ridiculous. There is no question of anyone wanting to take your child. This is simply a matter of you both accompanying me to Sicily so that the legal complexities of a certain situation can be dealt with. All that is involved is a stay of a week—ten days at the most—and then you will be free to return here if that is your wish. I give you my word on that.'

Julie looked at him. His giving of 'his word' should have sounded theatrical, something for her to question and even mock, but somehow instead she found herself reacting to his words at some deep psychological level—as though a contract had been made, a promise given, a vow, almost. She could feel her breath leaking from her lungs and she knew that the slight inclination of her head was an acknowledgement of that contract—just as powerful a commitment from her as his words had been from him.

She had relaxed slightly, but a woman like this one, who had no conception of honour or what was due to a man's given word, was all too likely to cause the kind of public display she had already tried to cause once, Rocco decided, making up his mind that the sooner they were on their way to Sicily the better. Since she had their passports with her, he could see no sense in prolonging their departure. His personal jet was on standby, with its flight path filed. There was nothing to be gained by delaying things. Once she was in the car, she could argue with him all she wanted.

'Now, if we can both get into the car and out of this rain,' Rocco continued, opening the passenger door of the car for her.

Julie was still hesitating.

'I assure you that, far from suffering any harm, as you seem to think, ultimately both you and the child stand to benefit financially,' Rocco told her coolly.

Benefit? Financially? What did that mean? Julie's heart started to beat too fast.

Ah, now he had found the key to unlock her resistance, Rocco thought cynically.

'But why? I mean, I know that your brother...' She could not bring herself to say that she knew that his brother might be Josh's father, because that meant admitting to herself that Josh might not be James's son, and she longed so much for it to have been James who had fathered him, even though Judy herself had told her that she was not completely sure about who the father was. It was Josh she must think of now, though, she warned herself, and if the family of the wealthy playboy with whom her sister had had a fling were prepared to make some kind of financial provision for Josh, what right did she have to deny her nephew that benefit?

A fresh fear struck her. What if Antonio Leopardi wanted to claim Josh and take him from her? What if that was what this was all about?

The car, long, shiny and expensive, was parked beneath a streetlight, and she could see quite plainly the contemptuous look in the slightly hooded golden-amber eyes as he turned towards her. The eyes of a predatory hunter. Leopard's eyes.

'Antonio was my half-brother, not my brother. He was Sicilian, therefore this child—his child—is also Sicilian, and as such is entitled to his inheritance. That is the law of our blood and our family.'

The whole sentence was seamed with warnings as dark and ancient as Sicily's own history, but initially it was the first three words he had spoken that Julie focused on.

'Antonio *was* Sicilian?' she repeated. 'What does that mean?'

'It means exactly what it always means when one speaks of a person's life in the past tense,' Rocco told her curtly. 'My half-brother—your lover, the child's father—is dead. However, whilst the Leopardi family does not have another Antonio, and most certainly will not supply you with a replacement lover—' another even more derisory look, designed to strip whatever pride she might have left from her much in the same manner that one of his ancestors might have ordered that a criminal be flayed alive, followed the first one '—it does take its responsibilities towards those of its blood very seriously.'

She was almost mentally and emotionally numb now, as well as numb with cold, and the hardship of these last months was abruptly taking its toll on her. It was hard to remember now that she had ever been a confident, successful young woman, with a promising career in local government in front of her—never mind that it was less than six months since she had been smartly turned out, well fed, a stone heavier, with glossy hair and a growing circle of new acquaintances, sharing a comfortable apartment with three other young female graduates who, like her, had jobs in local government.

The thought of sharing the responsibility for the safe upbringing of the child she loved so much with a proper family, with a man with shoulders broad enough to carry that weight easily and safely, filled her with unexpected relief. How much easier all those decisions that would need to be made down through the years would be if there were others to share them with her, for her to turn to, others who—unlike James's sister—would not reject her nephew.

Rocco Leopardi might not reject Josh, but he was making it plain what he thought of *her*, and instinctively Julie wanted to defend herself and refute his accusations. She began to say indignantly,

'But I am not—' and then wondered if it would be wise to tell him that she was not Josh's mother. He might have given her his word that she and Josh would not be separated, but that word had been given to her as Josh's mother, not his aunt—even if, as his aunt, she was also his legal guardian. Julie had no idea why she felt the need to conceal her true relationship to Josh, only that instinctively somehow she did.

'You're not what? Distraught at the thought of Antonio's death? No, I can see that,' Rocco observed as he held open the car door for her to get in. 'But then it was hardly a long-standing relationship that you had with him, was it?'

As she sank into the luxury of the blissfully comfortable seat Julie dipped her head, knowing that she now had to either accept his insults or confess that she wasn't Josh's mother.

'What happened to…to Antonio?' Julie had no

idea why she was asking. She had not even known the man, after all, even if the news of his death had come as a shock.

'He died as he lived,' Rocco told her curtly. 'Believing that nothing and no one mattered apart from himself.'

Now Julie looked at him, taken aback by the contempt she could see in his gaze.

'He was showing off, driving a car he did not have the skill to control far too fast.'

Judy had said that she and Antonio were two of a kind, and from what Rocco had just told her it sounded as if she had been right, Julie acknowledged.

'However, if the child is of our blood,' Rocco continued curtly, 'then no matter how carelessly he was conceived he is of us—a part of us, Leopardi.'

Instinctively Julie wanted to tell him that there was no way Josh could be a Leopardi, and that it was James who was his father. She had been so determined to believe that Josh was James's son that she was still in shock from the sudden appearance of Rocco Leopardi, with his unwanted reminder that not even her sister had known just who Josh's father was.

The look in the leopard eyes whilst he had been speaking had been all fiercely proud severity and intent. He really meant what he was saying, Julie recognised. His words revealed to her the centuries-old proud belief of a family who prized their blood and honoured their responsibility towards it above everything and everyone else.

It was slowly beginning to sink in for her just what it would mean if Josh *was* Antonio Leopardi's son. A part of her wanted to state that she knew beyond any shadow of a doubt that Antonio could not be Josh's father—but, even if Rocco Leopardi would accept that claim, how much damage might she be doing to Josh if she were to deny him his right to a heritage that might be his?

It was his need and his well-being that she must put first from now on, until the day came when he was old enough to make such a decision for himself. After all, she loved him for himself equally as much as she loved the thought of him being James's son.

Just as she could not and must not refuse to go to Sicily and reject whatever financial advantage for Josh that visit might bring about, so equally she must not deny the fact that he could be, as Rocco Leopardi has so emotively put it, 'of Leopardi blood'.

It was obvious that Rocco Leopardi did not know about her sister's death and thought that she was Judy. Julie's lips twisted in a small sad smile. If he had known her sister he would never have mistaken them. Both of them had disliked the fact that their parents had chosen such similar names for them, but it had been Judy who had complained about it most frequently when they had been growing up, stating that it was silly when they were so different and she was so much prettier and more popular than Julie.

'What will happen when we reach Sicily?'

'Our family doctor will do a DNA test.'

'But that could have been done here,' Julie protested.

Ignoring her outburst, Rocco continued, 'It will be at least five days before it is possible to have the results of this test. If it should prove that the child was fathered by Antonio then naturally that will mean that your son is part of our family.'

'And if they do not prove that?' Julie asked

huskily, unable to bring herself to look at him as she made what she knew in Rocco Leopardi's eyes would be an admission of her lack of morals.

Rocco frowned. Her behaviour was not what he had expected. He had anticipated that her manner would be more coy—cloyingly so— with many protestations of love for Antonio and her conviction that her child *must* be his half-brother's. It seemed out of character that she should talk so openly about the possibility of the child not being Antonio's.

'Then you will be financially recompensed for agreeing to travel to Sicily and given a substantial sum of money in return for your discretion.'

Julie's eyes widened.

'You mean that you will buy my silence?' she guessed shrewdly, watching as Rocco inclined his head in agreement.

How unpalatable and sleazy the whole situation was, Julie thought uncomfortably. She wished desperately that she and Josh did not have to be part of the whole unpleasant situation, but for Josh's sake she had to ignore her own distaste.

'Of course if you already know the father is not Antonio…?'

'No, I can't be sure,' Julie had to admit.

She was telling the truth, Rocco recognised.

The interior or the car smelled of expensive leather mixed with a hint of equally expensive male cologne. Julie turned to look at her sleeping nephew, thankful that she had taken the time to feed and change him before she had left the nursery.

Josh was such a quiet baby. Too quiet, Julie often worried, and the lovely new doctor at their busy local practice had agreed when Julie had raised her concerns with her.

Initially Julie hadn't wanted to betray her dead sister by telling the doctor that she had often worried that Judy neglected her baby, but Josh's health was her responsibility now, and more important to her than any loyalty she might owe a sister whose attitude to life had been opposite to her own and who had often treated her so unkindly.

The sad truth was—as Julie had feared and the doctor had gently confirmed—that poor little Josh had been neglected and malnourished by his mother during the first weeks of his life. Because the infection he had picked up had been left untreated it had compromised his immune system, which had then struggled to combat the winter viruses other babies could throw off. Emotionally too he had suffered—from maternal neglect. Julie had sworn to herself that she would make up for the sad early weeks of his life, and ideally she would have liked to be with him herself twenty-four-seven. But that, of course, was not possible since they were dependent on her income until her parents' estate was settled.

Slowly Josh had started to recognise her and respond, and earlier in the week for the very first time he had smiled at her and held out his arms to be picked up. Just thinking about that precious, wonderful moment now as she looked at him brought a lump of emotion to Julie's throat.

Everything about this car was expensive and new and clean, including the baby seat, and so very different from the shabby second-hand things that were all she had been able to afford once she had realised that many of those to whom her sister had owed money expected *her* to pay off her sister's debts.

Rocco started the car's engine and eased away from the pavement, causing Julie to look at him and demand, 'What are you doing?'

'I'm driving us to the airport,' he told her with exaggerated patience, 'where we shall board a plane to take us home to Sicily.'

Sicily? Now? When she didn't have so much as a change of clothes for Josh, never mind herself, and she hadn't even agreed that they would go—at least not properly.

'We can't do that,' Julie protested wildly.

'Why not?' Rocco asked her.

'There are things I need to do, people I need to tell—my landlord, and the crèche, and where I work. And we...Josh needs...we both need clothes and...and his...'

'You can telephone everyone you need to speak with here from the car. As for everything that the child might need, you may leave that to me.'

Quite plainly he was a man who did not like wasting time, Julie thought weakly, her eyes widening as Rocco pressed a button on the steering wheel of his car and a mobile phone slid out from the dashboard.

It gave Julie a feeling rather like deliberately swimming out of her depth to make the phone calls which were in effect committing her to accompanying Rocco to Sicily.

She was just finishing leaving a halting explanation on the message service at the crèche when
a small whimper from the back of the car had her
concluding her message quickly, so that she
could turn to look at Josh, who was now awake
and grizzling.

'Could you stop the car, please?' she asked
Rocco, elaborating when he frowned, 'I want to
sit in the back with Josh.'

Rocco had pulled over almost before she had
stopped speaking, getting out of his own seat whilst
she was still unfastening her seat belt to come
round to her door and open it for her. He placed his
hand beneath her elbow as he helped her out.

His manners certainly could not be faulted,
Julie admitted, along with his kissing technique.
They were in a class of their own.

Julie froze, hardly daring to breathe, the blood
suddenly flooding her face in a rich tide of guilty
colour. What on earth had made her think that?
She felt shocked and mortified, reduced by her
own confusion to stammering slightly as Rocco
opened the rear passenger door of the car for
her, allowing her to get inside.

She couldn't—dared not—look at him, so she

busied herself instead with removing her coat and fussing over Josh, who had stopped crying now but was still awake, whilst from the front of the car she could hear Rocco speaking in what she assumed must be Italian, using the hands-free phone she herself had just used.

As he explained to an exclusive concierge service exactly what he wanted, Rocco watched Julie discreetly in his rearview mirror, and then frowned. He hadn't expected her to be as devoted to her child as she obviously was. That, like the fear of him she had displayed earlier, sat uncomfortably with his pre-assessment of her.

Only now that the decision was made, and its execution taken out of her hands, could she admit to herself how exhausted she felt, Julie admitted. The debilitating and often frightening feeling that it would be easier to crawl than walk, easier to lie down than do either, had been growing steadily these last few months, inexorably stalking her until at times she came face to face with it and realised how much stronger and more powerful it was than her.

The peace and comfort of the car, along with its steady movement, were lulling her to sleep, but she must not give in to her aching need to close her eyes. She must think of Josh. She must put his needs first....

Rocco glanced in his driving mirror to see if Julie was still asleep. It was nearly an hour now since he had seen her eyes close, and she had fallen asleep with the speed of a child. But even in sleep her hand rested protectively on the side of the baby carrier. No one else could touch it or the child in it without waking her, Rocco suspected.

The smell of cheap wet wool being warmed by the car's heating system reached his nostrils. His fastidious eldest brother would quickly have shown his displeasure, Rocco reflected, but he was more down to earth. In the construction industry one had to be.

His father had been furious when he had learned what Rocco planned to do with the land left to him by his mother's uncle. A resort with its own private airfield on what should have been Leopardi land—it was unthinkable, an abomination, a betrayal of everything that the name Leopardi stood for: tradition, continuation of the male line, pride and secrecy.

'On my *mother's* land,' Falcon had corrected his father, stepping in to shield his younger sibling from their father's wrath, just as he had done so many times during their childhood.

They said that blood was thicker than water, but it was the Leopardi blood he shared with his brothers to which Rocco was loyal—not the Leopardi blood of his father.

The lights of the airport, gleaming on the wet tarmac, shone up ahead of them through the winter night, and as Rocco brought the car's speed down Julie woke up, not knowing just where she was for a few seconds, and then—when she did—looking anxiously at Josh, relieved to see that he was still asleep before glancing self-consciously towards the front of the car. She could see Rocco's hands resting on the steering wheel, and for some reason the sight of them made her heart jerk against her ribs. It was an effort to drag her gaze away from him to look out of the car window instead.

They were turning off the main access road, swinging round down a smooth road and up to a checkpoint, where Rocco produced a plastic card for the security guard—who saluted him before raising the barrier.

The car picked up speed, and Julie's eyes widened in disbelief as she realised that, no, she wasn't seeing things. Rocco *was* driving right up to the sleek silver jet parked on the tarmac in front of them.

'Good evening, sir.'

Rocco smiled at Nigel Rowlins, the first officer of his private jet, as he opened the door of the Mercedes.

'Good evening, Nigel. All set to go, are we?'

'Yes, indeed, sir. Flight plan's logged and approved, the deliveries have arrived and have been loaded. Passport control's on alert.'

Rocco nodded his head.

They were flying to Sicily in a private jet? Why hadn't she realised that that might be the case? Because she wasn't used to people whose life-style included private jets, that was why, Julie answered her own question wryly.

She had been banking on them going through the departure area so that she could at least buy some necessities for Josh—luckily his bottles and heater were in the nappy bag, along with a couple of changes of clothes. And she needed a change of clothes for herself—the cheaper the better, since she only had a tiny bit of cash on her. Now what was she going to do? She realised that Rocco Leopardi had said that he would deal with things, but she neither expected nor wanted to him to buy anything for them. There was no way she wanted to feel beholden to him. No way at all.

Perhaps he had forgotten what he had said? Perhaps she should remind him?

She took a deep breath and said quietly, 'I was hoping we'd have some time to buy clothes.'

The soft, quiet voice was at odds with the intent behind her words—which said quite plainly that she'd been expecting him to take her on a shopping spree.

'You will find everything you are likely to need is already on board,' Rocco told her dismissively.

'Everything?' Julie queried uncertainly. How could that be? He hadn't so much as asked her what Josh might need.

'Everything.' Rocco confirmed grimly. What was she expecting? *Carte blanche* at Heathrow's duty-free designer shops? Tough, he decided unsympathetically as he got out of the car, effectively putting an end to their conversation, and going to open the door nearest to Josh. He reached in to lift him out of the baby seat, leaving Julie to gather together her coat, the baby bag and her own handbag, and follow him out onto the tarmac.

It was dark now, and cold, causing Julie to shiver.

The shock of the cold air after the warmth of the car woke Josh, and his thin, fretful cry jerked on Julie's heartstrings. It was too cold for him out here, and he needed feeding.

Rocco Leopardi was still holding Josh. Turning away from her, he strode towards the plane, taking the steps two at a time with easy, relaxed energy, leaving her no option other than to hurry after him.

If the uniformed steward waiting in the luxuriously furnished cabin was surprised by her appearance, or the fact that his boss was holding a shabbily dressed crying baby, he was too well trained to show it, simply offering to take Julie's coat from her and asking her what she would like to drink.

'Something hot rather than something alcoholic, Russell,' Rocco Leopardi was answering on her behalf, and the fact that he was not allowing her to make her own decision filled Julie with an unfamiliar and foolish desire to insist that actually she wanted champagne, even though in reality she rarely touched alcohol.

Instead she gave the steward a diffident smile and asked uncertainly, 'If there is somewhere to heat Josh's bottle?'

'Of course. I've got a choice of formula in the galley for when you want it, and the cot and everything else has been set up in the sleeping cabin.'

'It's no wonder he looks so whey-faced and undersized, since you obviously aren't feeding him yourself.'

Rocco's criticism, voiced the moment the steward had disappeared with the bottle Julie had removed from the shabby nappy bag, caused her to stare at him. The colour came and went in her face as she searched and failed to find a response that would have the effect of putting him in his place and ensuring that he knew just how seriously she took her responsibilities towards Josh.

'I have to go out to work,' was all she could think of to say, and she prayed that he wouldn't make any comment about expressed breast milk being better than formula.

Ignoring her response, he continued, 'As Russell just said, you'll find everything you need in the inner cabin. It will be a three-hour flight, so feel free to snatch a couple of hours' sleep yourself, if you wish.' He frowned when he saw the wariness in her eyes, demanding, 'What's that look for? You are perfectly safe. I can assure you that I'm not desperate enough to lower myself to make use of Antonio's leavings.'

Dangerously, the repugnance in his voice actually hurt her. Why? There had only ever been one man she had wanted to desire her, and that had been James. He *had* desired her—until Judy had bewitched him and taken him from her. She certainly didn't desire Rocco Leopardi, and she never would.

The steward had reappeared.

'We'll be taking off soon,' he told her. 'If you'd like to come with me, we've got a sky cot set up for the baby in the sleeping compartment.'

Obediently, Julie turned towards the door he was indicating. That was the trouble with her, James had once told her. She was far too responsible and law-abiding, What he had meant, of course, was that compared to Judy—who had been spectacularly good at taking risks and getting away with taking them—she was dull and boring.

But she was also alive, Julie reminded herself sadly, whilst Judy, James and two sets of loving parents were all dead. And all because Judy had wanted a big candyfloss wedding in a fairy-tale castle. The same castle where a well-known glamour model celebrity had married.

As the steward opened the door into the sleeping compartment, Julie saw that Rocco Leopardi was busy working on a computer which had appeared almost magically at the touch of a button on the desk in front of him.

What the steward had referred to as a sleeping 'compartment' was far from being the utilitarian and small space Julie had imagined. It was, in fact, the most luxurious bedroom she had ever seen.

Thick pale-coloured carpet covered the floor, merging with equally pale walls. The bed—surely the widest Julie had ever seen, and equally surely, she decided, with distaste, intended for the sort of sex games and romps her sister had freely and boastfully indulged in rather than merely for a good night's sleep—barely filled a third of the floor space.

'The controls for the bed are here,' the steward was telling her. 'You can raise it to read or watch TV.' He pressed several buttons on the remote he was holding in demonstration, causing one half of the bed to tilt up as though it were a chair, whilst almost magically a huge TV screen appeared from a narrow cupboard on the opposite wall.

'We've set up the sky cot here,' he added. 'Right next to the seat you'll need to strap yourself into for take-off and landing. It pulls down out of the wall, like so. The bathroom and dressing room are through that door next to the bed. I've unpacked a few things for you and the baby, and hung them up. I'll be serving dinner in about half an hour. If Rocco follows his normal form he'll want to work as soon as he's had dinner, so you might want to think about getting a few hours' sleep. We'll be landing shortly before one in the morning. I don't know what the baby's exact routine is, but I shall be on standby if you need me for anything. I'll bring the heated milk as soon as we're airborne.'

Julie would have liked to tell him that she'd rather eat her food on her own, and as far away from Rocco Leopardi as possible, but she didn't—because she didn't want to cause the steward any extra work.

A light above the door started to flash.

'Take-off,' the steward told her briskly.

Two minutes later Josh was strapped into his sky cot and Julie into her seat.

CHAPTER TWO

'HERE'S the baby's milk, and I've brought you a pot of tea.'

Julie nodded her thanks to the steward. Their take-off had been smooth, but even so it had left Josh fretful, and he was grizzling as Julie lifted him out of the sky cot to feed him. She tested the heat of the formula and then settled down with him. At first he sucked greedily, but then to her dismay he suddenly rejected the teat, crying in pain and drawing his legs up towards his body.

He was having an attack of colic, Julie recognised anxiously as she tried to comfort him, gently rubbing his torso the way the doctor had shown her.

To her relief, almost immediately he started to relax. The disruption to his routine meant that this feed was late. He must have been so hungry, poor baby, that he'd tried to take it too fast. He was tired as well.

Ten minutes later, when he had only managed a third of the bottle, Julie admitted defeat, putting the bottle to one side and lifting him against her shoulder to wind him. Almost immediately he was sick, covering both himself and Julie's jumper with sour-smelling sticky formula.

He was crying again now, and Julie felt a bit like crying herself. It was so important that he got the nourishment he needed, but the attacks of colic he suffered meant that feeding times had become a nightmare of anxiety for her—even though the doctor had assured her that she was doing everything correctly.

He felt so light. Lighter than he had yesterday? Was he losing weight instead of gaining it?

She'd have to change him and then try again, Julie acknowledged, replacing the bottle in the thoughtfully provided insulated container before carrying Josh through into the bathroom.

Mirrored walls gave back to her an unprepossessing and unwanted image of her own too-thin body and wan face. The pair of them looked half-starved, pinched, and with too-sharp features, she admitted, as she stripped off Josh's soiled clothes and placed him down on his changing mat.

To her astonishment, the steward had told her that there were clean baby clothes and nappies in the drawers in the dressing room, along with clothes for herself. How Rocco Leopardi had managed to arrange that she had no idea—but perhaps when you were a Leopardi everything was possible. She suspected that Rocco would believe that being a Leopardi meant that it *should* be possible.

It would be a long time before she could forget the feel of those hard hands on her body, and even longer—if ever—before she could forget the feel of his mouth on hers. As an adult woman who earned her own living, she found the thought of wearing clothes bought for her by someone else made her body stiffen in angry rejection—but, whilst she might be able to afford the luxury of pride and self-denial for herself, she couldn't do that to Josh.

When she found the carefully folded baby clothes she looked at them with a mixture of anger and pain. Designer label baby clothes. What a shocking waste of money. All Josh or indeed any baby needed, surely, was simply clothes that were warm and clean and fitted? Even so, it was hard to stop herself from drawing in a small breath of delight as she removed a complete matching set of baby boy's clothes in soft blue, cream and beige. The little shirt had an identifiable designer check, the beige trousers were vaguely 'cargo' style, and the cardigan was blue and trimmed again with the same check— like the socks that completed the outfit. Even the babygro to go under everything had its own designer logo, and the disposable nappies were not only the right size, but were also 'boy' nappies—a luxury she had never been able to afford, and which she had told herself was little more than a cynical marketing ploy designed to add yet another expense to being a parent.

It was impossible to even think of touching such exquisite clothes whilst she was still wearing her formula-encrusted jumper—which, of course, would have to be washed and somehow dried in time for her to put it back on before she left the plane.

In the bathroom, Josh had started to cry. Quickly Julie pulled the jumper over her head. She needed a shower every bit as much as Josh needed a bath, so she might as well remove her skirt and her tights as well.

If there was one thing Josh did enjoy it was his bath, and with all the splashing around he did she'd be better off bathing him wearing only her bra and knickers.

It was amazing what wealth could do: nothing that Josh might need had been forgotten—right down to a baby bath and luxury products that smelled deliciously of vanilla.

Lifting Josh out of the bath, Julie wrapped him in a towel and carried him through into the bedroom, where she finally managed to coax him to take a bit more of his formula.

He was falling asleep as she put a clean nappy on him and then fastened him into a brand-new, deliciously soft sleep suit patterned with floppy-eared rabbits.

Kissing him tenderly, she put him in the sky cot, making sure that he was secure and safe before returning to the bathroom, where she washed out her jumper, cleaned up the baby bathtime mess, and then finally—blissfully—stepped into the shower.

In the main salon, Rocco finished writing the e-mail he was sending his elder brother and then tapped the 'send' button, mentally reviewing the events that had led to the search for Antonio's child.

Rocco hadn't planned to spend Christmas with his father and his brothers. He'd intended to fly to Colorado to stay with friends and ski, but then his eldest brother had telephoned him with the news that their father was terminally ill, so Rocco had flown home instead.

Home. Rocco lifted his arms to link his hands behind his head, exhaling as he did so. He was naturally strongly built, but the hard physical labour he had done during his teenage years, when he had preferred to work on a building site during his summer holidays rather than be financially tethered to his father, had honed and developed his muscles in a way that had left a legacy Rocco's tailors deplored and his lovers adored. Happily, one of the benefits of being a billionaire was that he could afford to have his shirts handmade and made to measure, to accommodate the powerful muscles of his chest and upper arms.

Falcon, aesthete that he was, tended to look down his long, proud nose at what he somewhat derisorily termed Rocco's 'prize fighter torso'. Alessandro, his second brother, was less critical.

'Who says that Father is dying?' Rocco had asked Falcon cynically. 'Because if it is the old man himself…'

'It isn't. I've spoken to the specialist myself. He gives Father a year at the most. I see no point in any of us pretending that we're grief stricken,' Falcon had continued coolly. 'At least here amongst ourselves we can be open and honest without being judged as uncaring.'

From the high windows of the ancient fortress that had been their childhood home it was possible—just—to see the summit of Mount Etna. Etna, like their father, breathed bellicosity, fire and danger—and like their father it was a symbol of power. The kind of power that could be cruel and destructive.

Their father's power, though, was waning, if Falcon was to be believed, and his eldest brother had never given Rocco reason to do anything other than believe him.

It had been a solemn moment. Their father—the head of one of Sicily's greatest, most powerful and rich aristocratic dynasties—was dying.

At thirty-four, a billionaire in his own right via his own endeavours, and the least loved and favoured of his father's three living sons, Rocco acknowledged that he should have been the last person to be swayed by the deathbed plea of a man who had spent his entire adult life manipulating others to his own will, and who was responsible for the death of Rocco's own mother. No more children, their father had been told after the births of Falcon and Alessandro, but he had ignored that warning, and his delicate wife had died within hours of giving birth to her third son.

Her death had left a bitterness and a canker at the heart of the family, dividing father and sons, and that bitterness had been driven deeper when their father had married his long-term mistress within a year of their mother's death.

However, tradition was burned deep into the hearts of the Leopardi family, handed down from generation to generation from the time when the Saracens had been driven from the land by the Normans and the first Leopardi had taken as his wife the daughter of the Saracen lord who had owned the vast, rich tracts of land that had passed with her to her husband. Those traditions involved putting the family and what was best for it first, rather than any individual member. They had held fast and become so tightly woven into the Leopardi culture that they were bred into their blood and souls.

As Falcon had said after he had spoken with them, despite their lack of love for their dying father they could not simply turn their backs and walk away from the duty he had imposed on them all.

They had been summoned to their father's bed-chamber—a lofty, feudally styled room, hung with the banners of past battle glories—where their father had been lying almost in state in the vast double bed.

It had been in this bed that they had all been con-ceived, including Antonio, their late half-brother—who, if their father was to be believed, had confided to him before he died that he had fathered a child.

'There is a child—born to an Englishwoman. And that child is a Leopardi.'

Their father's long thin fingers had curled round the silver head of his cane and he'd rapped it hard on the floor.

'It is Leopardi and Sicilian by its father's blood. He or she belongs here at Castello Leopardi, with this family.'

'And the mother of this child?' Alessandro had asked.

'Antonio did not have time to say her name.'

Rocco remembered thinking that Antonio probably hadn't even been able to remember it.

The old Prince's retort had been typical of his way of thinking and his way of life. 'This woman, in carrying Antonio's child and keeping it from us, his family, is guilty of theft. The child must be brought here. It is his birthright and ours. Antonio was my son.'

And his most beloved son. They had all known that.

'This child belongs here. It was Antonio's dying wish to me that this should be so.'

'Having no doubt refused flatly to accept any responsibility whatsoever for it during his lifetime, knowing our dear late half-brother as we do,' Alessandro had murmured dulcetly to Rocco, out of earshot of their father.

'That is all very well, Father, but we do not know the identity of the mother of Antonio's child,' Falcon had reminded their father, 'since Antonio neglected to tell you her name.'

Their father had refused to listen.

'The child must be found.'

That had been the Prince's living will and his dying demand, and in the end they had had no honourable option as Leopardis other than to concede defeat.

Two weeks later they had all been back in their father's bedchamber, to hear the results of the investigations Falcon had put in hand.

'We now know that out of the multitude of women Antonio appears to have disported himself with last summer, only one went on to have a child,' Falcon informed them all. 'This woman was a British holidaymaker, attending the Cannes Film Festival at the time. Not entirely surprising, since Antonio had a taste for a combination of blonde hair and loose morals. However, there is no guarantee that it is this child to which Antonio was referring. It is true that it was conceived at the right time, but the only way we can be sure that the child is Antonio's is via a DNA test, and for that we shall need the mother's co-operation. In my view the simplest thing would be to approach the mother and—'

'The child belongs here.' Their father had interrupted Falcon angrily. 'But only the child. The mother is nothing—little more than a slut who tempted and tormented my poor son until in his craziness his life was stolen from him and he was stolen from me. My beloved and most precious child—your brother. Your youngest brother. Where were you when he needed protecting from this harlot, whoever she is? You, Falcon, were in Florence, presiding over copyists and their fake works of art. You, Alessandro, were buying yet more jets for your airline—and you, Rocco, were too busy overseeing the rebuilding of Rome in the middle of the desert, for tourists to go and gawp at. No doubt flown there by your brother's airline and decorated by Falcon's copyists.'

They had all been aware of his angry contempt. But then they had all been aware of their father's contempt for them all their lives. They were, after all, the sons of the woman their father had been forced to marry against his will.

Oh, yes, their father had been passionate in his contempt for them—expending energy he did not have in his determination to inject every bit of passion and persuasion into his voice as he extracted from them their reluctant promise that they would find the Englishwoman who had carried their dead brother's child and that they would bring that child back to Sicily to be raised as a Leopardi.

Antonio himself could not be restored to their father since he was dead—killed in a senseless, stupid accident, showing off in his new car. So typical of him and so unacceptable to their father, who had adored the son of his second wife—the woman who had been his mistress during his marriage to their own mother.

If Falcon was right—and given Antonio's well-known and well-documented taste in downmarket females, he probably was—the mother of his child would pretty soon recognise the commercial value of her child, and would want to take full advantage of that fact.

The Leopardi men might not publicly boast about their high social status or their wealth, but that did not alter the fact that both existed.

As a first step toward ascertaining if the child was Antonio's, it had been agreed that the mother would have to be persuaded to allow the child to undergo DNA tests, without being allowed access to either the press or a lawyer whilst they were awaiting the results.

All three brothers had agreed that until such time as the child had either been confirmed as Antonio's or proved not to be, the mother must be kept secluded from any contact with others— either voluntarily or, more feasibly, given the type of woman she would be, not voluntarily.

'You mean we shall have to bring this woman to Sicily and keep her here until we have ascertained whether or not Antonio was the father of her child?' Alessandro had asked Falcon, frowning disapprovingly as he did so.

Falcon had simply shrugged aside his brother's distaste, stating coolly, 'Unless you have a better idea?'

None of them had, but Rocco had had another issue with which he was not happy.

'Our father has stated that it is the child he wants, but not the mother, so that it can be raised as a Leopardi. Apart from the damage it could do to a child to be deprived of any contact with its mother, given the way Antonio turned out—'

'You are worrying unnecessarily, Rocco,' Falcon had told him. 'Our father's life expectancy is limited. It is true that he is not quite as close to death's door as he would have us think—he could have another year—but ultimately it is us who will decide the future of this child, if it should be Antonio's. I assure you that I share your feelings with regard to the child's mother. Whatever decision is made about the child's future, that future will include its mother. You have my word on that and so will she. No child should grow up without its mother.'

They had all looked at one another. Rocco knew how badly the death of their mother had affected both his brothers. However, it wasn't true that he himself had no knowledge of her. She had after all carried him close to her heart for nine months, and he had been born knowing that—knowing too that he had lost her.

'And if this child is not Antonio's?' Alessandro had asked.

'Then she will be recompensed for her co-operation—and her future silence regarding this debacle,' Falcon had answered.

'It is damnable that our father should impose this duty on us,' Alessandro had said angrily.

'Damnable, indeed. But we shall be damned if

we do not accept the duty imposed on us by our father. The duty to accept such a charge—father to son—came to us with our conception. It is encoded in our genes. We cannot change that any more than we can change our inherited bone structure or the blood that runs through our veins. Antonio's child, if he or she exists, is of those genes and therefore of us. We have a duty and a responsibility towards it that goes beyond any promise we have made our father.'

Who could argue with that? Not him, Rocco admitted now, although he *had* argued—and very passionately—with Falcon's announcement that since he had commitments overseas he could not escape, and because Alessandro was in the middle of negotiating tricky new contracts for his airline business it would fall to Rocco to go to London and persuade this Julie Simmonds to return to Sicily with him, bringing her child with her.

'Now, the first thing we need to do is persuade the woman to come to Sicily with her child, and...'

Rocco grimaced now, remembering how Falcon had paused and then looked at him.

'Me? Why me?' Rocco had objected, with a

lifetime's worth of a youngest sibling's indignation and resentment.

'I have just explained,' Falcon had pointed
out, adding firmly, 'In performing this task
you are carrying a heavy responsibility for all
of us, Rocco.'

Trust Falcon to make it sound as though he
had been awarded a prize instead of being
dumped on, Rocco thought grimly now. He
wasn't liking the 'duty' which, according to
Falcon, his genes imposed on him any more than
he had expected. Perhaps the streak of rebelli-
ousness within him that pulled against the iron
grip of the Leopardi family code was something
that had come down to him from his mother? She
had, after all, been only part-Sicilian. *Her*
father's family had come from Florence—the
city that Falcon loved so much.

Rocco glanced at his watch.

They had been in the air for close on an hour.
He was hungry and ready for his dinner. The
steward had assured him that he had told Julie
Simmonds when he would be serving their meal.
If she was one of those women who believed that
good time keeping was an unnecessary nuisance

that need not apply to her, she needed to have the error of her ways pointed out to her.

Rocco stood up and strode towards the bedroom door.

CHAPTER THREE

THE shower area of the bathroom was designed as a wet room, without any protective screen, and the water was blissfully hot and there was plenty of it. Such a treat after the miserable trickle of never more than lukewarm water that came from her own shower.

Julie acknowledged that she had stayed under its wonderful spray longer than perhaps she should, but even so it was still a shock when the bathroom door—which she hadn't thought to lock—was suddenly pulled open, and she saw Rocco Leopardi standing there, fully dressed, his gaze travelling slowly and deliberately the full length of her naked body. Such a shock, in fact, that Julie didn't even think to cover either her sex or her breasts until it was far too late and that gaze had swept all the way back up over her and come to rest on her flushed face.

'Well, well—a natural blonde. Now, that *is* a surprise,' Rocco drawled mockingly.

What was also a surprise, although he had no intention of feeding her vanity by saying so, was just how erotic he found the sight of the naturally neat rather than sleekly waxed tousle of damp blonde curls that clung to the gentle rise of her flesh, just above the sensually shaped and softly closed lips that concealed the inner intimacy of her sex.

Already, and against his own wishes, he could feel himself responding to what he could see.

She might be a natural blonde, but she was every bit as thin as he had suspected, he told himself, hoping to channel his thoughts into rejection of her rather than desire. Then, yes—but her breasts were far fuller than he had imagined, and natural too, perfectly shaped, with a full lower curve and nipples that tilted erotically upwards. A party girl's breasts, not a nursing mother's. In focusing on her sexuality she was depriving her child. But then a woman like her would do that, wouldn't she?

It had been her total abandonment to the sensual pleasure he had seen in every line of her body as she had stood naked beneath the shower, her face tilted up towards the water, her eyes closed and every inch of her flesh showing its joy, that was responsible for the hardening of his own flesh right now, Rocco acknowledged. Something about that abandonment made him want to walk into the shower and share it with her. It made him want to take her swiftly and hotly, his flesh sinking deep into hers, whilst her muscles closed around him, in a primitive shared physical orgy of greedy pleasure and hedonistic satisfaction. Like rough wine on a hot day after hard physical activity—the base, thoughtless satisfaction of a momentary fierce need.

If he did feel like that then he was a fool, Rocco told himself cynically. She was a piece of flesh that had no doubt been handed out to any number of other men before his brother, and would be handed out to others. That was her choice, and he certainly wasn't moralizing, but her type did nothing for him. Right now the only hunger he wanted to recognise was the hunger that was driving him, which came from his stomach and not from his loins, he told himself determinedly.

Reaching for a towel, he threw it towards her, telling her coolly, 'Russell is waiting to serve dinner. You've got five minutes. And let me warn you that my temper doesn't improve with hunger.'

Five minutes. Julie didn't even bother looking at the clothes which Russell the steward had said he'd hung in the wardrobe. She simply dried her body, plaited her wet hair, and then pulled on one of the thick white towelling robes she found hanging on the bathroom door.

She was out of breath and her heart was pounding when she slid into the chair that Rocco Leopardi pulled out for her.

'Four minutes and fifty-five seconds,' he commented as he went round to the other side of the elegantly set table and sat down.

If Rocco Leopardi found anything odd in the fact that she had chosen to eat wearing a bathrobe, he obviously wasn't going to say so. Which was just as well, Julie thought fiercely, because if he did she would tell him that it wasn't *her* choice that she was here on board his private jet, without a clean top to replace the one on which Josh had been sick.

It was, in fact, almost impossible to believe that they were actually on a plane and flying, Julie acknowledged, as she looked towards the bedroom door, which she had left propped open so that she could hear Josh if he woke up and started to cry.

Russell arrived with soup, putting Julie's down in front of her and then placing a linen napkin on her lap before she could do so herself.

The soup—lobster bisque—smelled heavenly. Julie couldn't remember the last time she had sat down to eat any kind of meal, never mind one like this, with beautiful napery and china, silver cutlery and Michelin-star-type food.

Russell was pouring them both a glass of wine. Julie looked at hers a little uncertainly. She wasn't a big drinker and, given that she hadn't eaten all day, alcohol on an empty stomach might not be a good idea.

'I dare say your tastes run more to Cristal?' Rocco said, seeing her expression and mistaking its cause.

Julie didn't bother to respond. She doubted he would believe her if she were to tell him that she had never even tasted Cristal champagne.

The soup was delicious, but very rich—too rich, Julie suspected, for her digestive system, which was more accustomed to baked beans on toast and porridge: cheap, filling food that somehow she never seemed to get the time to finish eating.

She took a quick sip of her wine and then wished she hadn't, when the alcohol went straight to her head.

If she was trying to impress him with her make-up-free face, and by wearing something that enveloped her from the neck virtually down to her ankles, she was wasting her time, Rocco thought grimly.

For one thing the bathrobe was gaping, so that every time she lifted her soup spoon he could see a bit more of the vulnerable curve of her throat and the soft pale skin below it, where her breasts lifted against the thick toweling, and for another he already had a perfectly recorded image of her standing naked beneath the shower imprinted on his memory.

The soup was good. Julie lifted another spoonful to her mouth and then paused, listening as she turned her head in the direction of the open bedroom door.

'Josh is awake,' she told Rocco, putting her spoon down. 'I'd better go to him. He might be hungry.'

'You've only just fed him,' Rocco pointed out as he too heard the thin, fretful cry from the bedroom.

'He's had a digestive problem which means that he needs small, regular feeds,' Julie told him.

Rocco frowned as he listened to her. 'Perhaps,' he pointed out, 'if you were less concerned about preserving your admittedly exceptionally well-shaped breasts and were feeding him as nature intended babies should be fed, he'd be more satisfied?'

Clearly her argument that she needed to work hadn't registered. Julie longed to tell him that his criticism was unfounded, but how could she without revealing the fact that she was not Josh's mother?

An unfamiliar feeling gathered inside her in a tense ball. A mixture of self-consciousness—she wasn't used to men commenting on the shape of her breasts—anxiety—she could hardly tell him *why* she wasn't breastfeeding—and something that had nothing to do with either of those feelings but instead had rather a lot to do with the knowledge that he had seen her naked, had her body responding to that fact. She hurried into the bedroom, glad of an excuse to escape from the table and the unwanted proximity of Rocco Leopardi.

Josh's fretful cry increased in volume the minute he saw her. At least now he recognised her and knew that she was the source of his food, Julie acknowledged, as she lifted him out of the travel cot. She'd have to ask Russell if she could use the galley to make Josh up a fresh bottle. She felt his nappy. He was dry and clean. She knew from experience that if she put him down he would get more upset and start to scream. Because Judy had often picked him up and then put him back down when he was hungry without feeding him? Her late sister had been the first to admit that she wasn't maternal, and that she had found the responsibilities of motherhood an onerous and unwanted burden.

Holding him against her shoulder, Julie popped a dummy in his mouth and carried him back to the main cabin, where Russell was clearing away their soup bowls.

'I need to make Josh a fresh bottle,' Julie told him.

'No problem,' he assured her. 'Everything is ready in the galley. I can't hold back the lamb cutlets much longer, though.'

'I don't want to interrupt your meal,' Julie told Rocco immediately. 'Josh can wait until it's been served, then I'll go and feed him in the other cabin.'

Her comment about the baby was made so naturally that it was impossible to accuse her of trying to score points, but at the same time it so directly opposed the selfish, non-maternal character he'd assigned her it made Rocco frown. He didn't like having his judgements challenged—especially when the person doing the challenging was himself.

'I rather think that Russell was thinking about your dinner as much as mine,' he told Julie succinctly, shaking his head as the steward reached for the wine bottle to refill his glass.

'Oh.' Julie smiled at the steward. A warm, natural smile that lit up her pale and thin face, illuminating it with the illusion—or was it the past shadow?—of a delicate, piquant beauty. 'That's kind of you, but I'm not really hungry.'

Russell nodded and headed back towards the galley.

He had just disappeared inside it when Josh spat out his dummy, his face creasing up as he started to cry.

'You'd better sort his food out,' Rocco announced. He had to raise his voice slightly over the sound of Josh's cries, and he wasn't looking very pleased.

Josh was probably getting on Rocco Leopardi's nerves, Julie thought, hugging the baby even more protectively. He was the kind of man—rich, powerful and no doubt spoiled— who wasn't used to having his wishes or himself taking second place to anything or anyone. No doubt when he had children they would be presented to their father only when he wished them to be. It would be someone else who would be there for the sleepless nights, the colic, and all the other exhausting aspects of parenthood.

He was the kind of man who would enjoy creating his children, though.

The thought slipped past the gates that should have barred it. Then, like a serpent, once it was there on the fertile ground from which it had been banished it luxuriated in its freedom and soon found a willing accomplice to listen to its dangerous story in the shape of a female instinct Julie hadn't even known she possessed until now.

It struck too swiftly for her to escape its

deadly venom. One minute she was picturing Rocco Leopardi as a selfish father—the next she was imagining him as an arrogantly sensual lover, wanting to impregnate his woman, wanting to make his mark on the future via the creation of a child that would carry his genes into that future with it.

Inside her head she could see the face of the woman, and in it her intense pleasure—*her* face.

Shock gripped her body in a violent tremor.

'I'll go through to the galley and sort out Josh's bottle,' Julie said, desperate to get away from Rocco even whilst she calmed her frantic thoughts. They ricocheted around inside her head in every direction in their flight to escape from what she had 'seen'.

Turning on her heel, she bolted for the galley, her heart jumping inside her chest in a panicky, unsteady rhythm that made her feel slightly sick.

'I'm really sorry about this,' she apologised to the steward as he looked up at her, 'but I think Josh is getting on Rocco's nerves. I thought I'd better come and do his bottle.' As she spoke she was measuring out the formula with practised ease, whilst holding Josh.

'No worries,' Russell reassured her calmly.

The lamb cutlets he was just sliding onto a serving dish decorated with wilted radicchio and mint leaves, before ornamenting them with white frilled 'caps', looked and smelled delicious, but Julie's anxiety about Josh had killed her appetite. She just hoped he would take his feed this time, and not have another attack of colic.

Josh was still crying when she carried him back to the bedroom, where she settled herself down in a chair with him and offered him his bottle.

Surely there was no sound more satisfying than the hungry sucking and assorted snuffling sounds made by a baby who was enjoying his feed? Julie thought, smiling when Josh gripped her finger tightly as she held the bottle and he held on to her. She stifled a small yawn, and then a much larger one. Josh released the teat of the bottle, and looked up at her, but then reached for it again when she made to take it away.

Five minutes later Julie could see that his eyelids looked as heavy with the desire to sleep as hers felt. He was only sucking drowsily now, his eyes tightly closed. Gently she eased the teat away, and then winded him gently before carrying him back to the cot.

Predictably, the minute she put him down his eyes opened wide and his face crumpled. 'It's all right. I'm not going anywhere,' she told him softly.

As though he understood what she was saying he started to relax, and then smiled at her, making her heart turn over with love.

She'd have to stay with him until he'd fallen asleep. She lifted her hand to her mouth to cover another yawn. She might as well lie down for a few minutes. She could see him from the bed, after all, and he could see her…

Rocco had finished his lamb cutlets, drunk his wine, shaken his head in refusal of pudding, and still Julie Simmonds had not re-emerged from the bedroom.

Rocco supposed irritably that he had better go and find out what was going on. He signalled to Russell to clear the table and strode over to the bedroom door, opening it and stepping inside the room, closing the door behind him.

A single lamp illuminated the room. Julie Simmonds was lying fast asleep on top of the bed, still wearing the bathrobe. If anything she looked even more fragile asleep than she did awake. She was lying with one arm outstretched, so that her hand was touching the side of the travel cot, as though even in her sleep her first concern was for her child. The towelling robe had fallen off her shoulder to reveal the fragility of her shoulder blade and its contrast with the soft fullness of her almost exposed breast.

An unfamiliar feeling shadowed Rocco's thoughts like the melancholic darkness of a deserted and lonely home. He had been born into one of the most patrician and wealthy of Sicilian families, but he had never known the kind of tender maternal love that this child was receiving.

From a mother who was little better than an unpaid whore and who was more concerned about preserving the sexuality of her future than feeding her child?

Was he really trying to tell himself that he was envious of that? So his mother had died within hours of his birth. He had at least been brought up with every material comfort and luxury, and his loss had taught him the value of emotional independence.

Rocco was about to turn away, when a movement from the cot caught his attention. The baby was awake, but quiet—and watching him, Rocco realised. It was impossible to see his features clearly in the shadowy room, but Rocco knew that the boy had dark curly hair, and that his eyes were still blue. He had felt no sense of looking at a child of his own blood. How could he, when as yet it was not known whether or not he was Leopardi? And yet somehow there was something—some feeling within himself, some deep awareness of a child's need to have a strong male protector and a man's need to honour his duty to be the guardian of a child's vulnerability—that called out to him as clearly as though the child himself had reminded him of that duty. Generation to generation, the responsibility was passed down, male to male, and when that golden chain of responsibility for the life of another was broken a small heart was left to bear the pain that was branded on it for ever: an imprint of what it was to be male, neither given nor received.

Someone had fathered this child; someone had to take responsibility for him.

Someone—but not him—not unless it turned out to be Antonio's child, and then he would share the responsibility with his brothers.

The baby wriggled and smiled a wide gummy smile. Rocco started to move closer to the cot and then stepped back, shaking off the primeval feelings that had no place in his logical mind and his busy life.

'We'll be landing in half an hour. Rocco said to warn you that it will be cold and possibly raining.'

'In Sicily?' Somehow Julie had assumed that the island would have warm weather all year round.

'The island faces three different seas, and its winters can be harsh. By the end of this month, though, the temperature will be rising and the weather will be much warmer.'

The steward's entrance had brought Julie out of her unplanned sleep.

He'd brought her a tray of tea when he'd come to wake her, and to warn her that they would soon be landing, but after he'd left her Julie was too busy to have time to pour and drink it.

For one thing Josh had to be changed, and fastened into clean clothes and a padded outdoor all-in-one suit before she could even think about getting ready herself. She doubted somehow that Rocco would have much patience if they delayed him.

To her dismay there was no sign of her wet jumper in the bathroom, or in fact of any of her own clothes, and there was certainly no time to go and find Russell and ask what had happened to them. Trying not to panic, Julie pulled open the wardrobe door, remembering that the steward had said he had hung her clothes there. Thankfully Josh was content to lie quietly as she stood staring at the things hanging inside the wardrobe, whilst her heart sank.

Designer jeans—she recognised the label as one that Judy had coveted—a silk shirt, a cashmere sweater, and a beautiful trench coat with a thick, warm removable lining swung invitingly in front of her. Timelessly elegant clothes, every single one of them way beyond her budget, never mind all of them together—and paid for by a man who had already shown his contempt for her. Wearing them would be a form of accepting his contempt, accepting his patronage, becoming a Leopardi possession—a woman who could be bought as easily as Antonio Leopardi had bought Judy—but what choice did she have? Her own clothes had vanished. She could hardly leave the plane wearing a towelling bathrobe—which in any case also belonged to Rocco Leopardi.

Almost fiercely she reached for the clothes and pulled them on, her angry movements softening the moment she touched the cashmere and the luxurious silk. It was a crime to treat such beautiful fabrics so harshly and uncaringly. The cashmere clung to the pads of her fingertips, slightly rough from all the domestic work she had to do without the luxury of protective gloves.

She had told herself that she wouldn't wear the expensive leather boots, but in the end she had to, when she found that her shoes had vanished along with everything else.

She was just folding the bathrobe when Russell knocked briefly on the door, and then came in carrying a butter soft suede bag of the type that Julie had seen A-list celebrity mothers toting.

'I've packed all the babe's things in it, and filled a fresh bottle. I'll make sure that everything else is sent on to Villa Rosa for you,' he told

Julie with a smile. 'Oh, and you'll need the raincoat.' He pulled a wry face. 'When it rains in Sicily in the winter, it really rains.'

She had her own nappy bag. Designer bags were an affectation and a waste of money, Julie told herself. But the butter-soft suede was already packed full. What was more important— her pride or Josh's comfort? There was no contest, really, was there?

When Julie emerged from the sleeping compartment carrying Josh, Rocco had to admit that the change in their appearance momentarily caught him off guard.

Julie still had her hair in a plait, and her face free of make-up, but somehow that simplicity only served to accentuate how perfectly suited she was to the stylish elegance of what she was wearing. Even the way she was carrying herself had altered, Rocco noted. She was standing taller, her shoulders straighter.

The concierge service had done an excellent job and he must remember to thank them. He had simply instructed them to make sure that enough clothes to last a young mother and her child for a fortnight, including both indoor and outdoor things, were sent to his private jet in time for their flight, along with adequate supplies of baby formula and other necessities.

If he said one word about the clothes he had bought, which she had been forced to wear, she would rip them off and refuse to leave the plane until she had her own clothes back, Julie decided defiantly, lifting her chin. She certainly wasn't going to thank him for them, was she? But somehow she heard herself saying huskily, 'Thank you for…for providing everything for Josh and me. You shouldn't have gone to so much trouble.'

Her voice made it plain that she was more resentful of his generosity than grateful, Rocco acknowledged grimly, and he told her, 'One phone call to a concierge service is hardly going to any trouble.'

He'd put his suit jacket back on, and over it he was wearing a raincoat with the collar turned up—with that special kind of aplomb and style that Italian men were so very good at.

A flashing light warned that their descent was about to begin, and broke the tension. Julie let Russell help her into her seat and fasten Josh into his, glad of the fact that their descent allowed her to escape from further conversation.

CHAPTER FOUR

IT WAS raining—hard. The rain bounced noisily off the umbrella that the steward was struggling to keep open over her against the fierce force of the wind as he escorted her to a waiting car, making sure she was safely inside it and settled comfortably in the rear with Josh in the baby seat before returning to the plane for Rocco.

The bright lights of the landing strip and the airfield illuminated a landscape that could have been anywhere: scrubby vegetation just visible beyond the perimeter fence under the flare of the lights, vanishing into an ink-black darkness that could have been land, sky or sea.

The cream leather upholstery of the car was so luxurious Julie was almost afraid of touching it. She looked at Josh, mentally praying that he would not be sick.

They were soon leaving the airfield and its

lights behind them, to be sucked into the rain-lashed darkness. Despite the warmth of the interior of the car, Julie shivered. The darkness was so intense it almost felt as though it was pressing in on the car, driven by the same wind that was forcing the rain against the car windows with a buffeting roar.

She didn't really know very much about Sicily, but she had never imagined it would be subject to this kind of violent weather.

Like a tightly wound spring, abruptly released to unravel too quickly, thoughts as wild as the night spun frantically through Julie's head. What if Rocco Leopardi's intentions towards Josh were not benign? What if Josh was an obstacle to him in some way? Why hadn't she thought of this before? Who would know—or care—if tonight she and Josh were driven away into the darkness never to return?

Reaction not just to the extraordinary events of the last few hours but also to everything else that had happened over the last few months and which she had refused to allow herself to react to—first for James's sake and then later for Josh's sake—hit her, smashing her self-control and thrusting her headlong into the grip of an attack of panic and self-blame so strong that it seized her breath and made her heart thump so heavily and with such speed that she thought it was going to burst out of her chest.

Rocco knew every centimetre of the single-track road that led from his private airstrip to Villa Rosa, one of the Leopardi country houses, but as always, as he drove round the final sharp curve in the road to reveal the villa up ahead, he felt the familiar surge of pride and pleasure at the sight of it, rising from the fertile plain to dominate the landscape with its elegance.

The sight of the villa materialising virtually out of the darkness, its honey-coloured walls illuminated by the large wrought-iron flambeaux that threw a soft flickering light not just over the building but also over the setting that housed it, brought Julie a merciful release from her anxiety.

Who could not look at something so stunningly architecturally beautiful and not be entranced by the sight of it?

'It's almost too perfect to be real.' Julie couldn't keep the awe from her voice as she stared up at the high portal, where what she assumed must be the Leopardi coat of arms was illuminated by the light of the flambeaux.

'It is real, I assure you,' Rocco drawled. 'It was built in the eighteenth century, originally as a summer retreat from the heat of the city. Caspar Leopardi designed it himself, and brought the very best craftsmen of the day here to work on it. He wanted to combine in the architecture all those things that were Leopardi—thus the front of the villa you see here is built on the classical lines of the eighteenth century, with reference to Greek and Roman architecture and thus the Greek and Roman influence on Sicily, whilst the enclosed courtyard around which the villa is built echoes the Arab influence on the island and on the Leopardi family.

'The flambeaux you can see here on the walls were especially commissioned on the island. Each one embraces a different part of our history via an heraldic design, and the gardens are of the Italianate style that was so popular amongst the English who travelled to Italy in the eighteenth century.'

As he spoke Rocco was driving them through

the portal to a formal courtyard dominated by an imposing marble stairway.

'The marble was quarried in Carrera,' Rocco told Julie, 'and the stairs lead up to the *piano nobile*—that is to say the main floor into the formal reception rooms of the villa.'

Julie's face burned with angry pride.

'I do know what *piano nobile* means,' she informed him sharply, but even if he realised he had offended her he certainly wasn't going to apologise, she recognised.

The emotional switchback she had been riding since he had stopped her in the street outside her flat, culminating as it just had with a surge of terror followed by an equally powerful release of that tension, was beginning to take effect on her body, Julie recognised muzzily. She had gone through too much, climbed too far too fast and fallen back too quickly, to maintain any equilibrium. She felt distinctly odd—weak, breathless, trembling inside, whilst her heart raced and thudded.

Rocco had brought the car to a halt in front of the double flight of stone stairs. His arrogant, 'I will take the child,' as he got out of the driver's seat, had Julie rushing feverishly to remove Josh from the baby seat, determined not to let him do so. She held her nephew tightly.

Instead of calming her, the sensation of the night air on her face made her feel slightly sick and dizzy. Holding on to Josh, she looked towards the flight of steps. So many of them, and she felt so very odd and weak—not like herself at all. Way above the porticoed entrance up at the top of the villa the carved stone heads of gargoyles and mystical animals stared down at her. All her growing doubts rushed in on her.

Why had she allowed him to persuade her to come here? Just as soon as she could she was going to demand some proper reassurances and explanations—and a lawyer to hear them, she told herself fiercely as she started to climb the stone steps.

She was halfway up them when it happened— her foot somehow slipping on the wet stone so that she half stumbled forward, with Josh in her arms.

Before she had time to cry out strong arms were gripping them, holding them both safe. She could smell male flesh—alien, and yet at the same time recognised by senses already attuned to him. She could feel male warmth, and had to fight to stop herself from simply wanting to relax into it, to give in to the weakness that had invaded her. She wanted to lie here against him, protected by him, never to have to leave that protection. She wanted his arms to close round her and stay closed round her. She ached almost desperately for a man like this one—a totally male, totally strong man—to lift the burdens she was carrying from her heart and heal the hurt inside her.

What was she thinking? The only man she had ever wanted—the only man she *would* ever want—was dead.

How long had passed? How many minutes had she been lying against him, her heart thumping sickly, too weak to move, whilst shocked tears of reaction and remorse blurred her vision? Too long.

If he hadn't been close enough and quick enough—if she had dropped Josh on the steps— if he had been hurt because of *her*...

'Give me the child. Unless, of course, you *want* to risk hurting him.'

He knew how to hurt her, she recognised. How to sense her weaknesses and use them against her.

Numbly, Julie handed the still-sleeping baby over to him.

It was Josh he wanted—just as it was for Josh's sake that he had saved her, not her own. And now that he had Josh he was striding up the stairs away from her, leaving her to follow on her own.

Out of nowhere a terrible lethargy rolled over her, accompanied by a bizarre longing to lie down and close her eyes. She looked up to the portico, her heart thumping ever harder. She could not climb the steps. She could not climb even one of them. But she must. Somehow, leaning against the stair wall for support, she managed to drag herself up one step and then another, closing her mind against the ache of pain in her legs.

Rocco took the steps two at a time, driven by the savage bite of his anger. Of all the stupid, irresponsible things to do.

She was a woman with pride.

What if he hadn't caught her in time?

She had defied him.

She had lain against him like a trapped fawn, too exhausted to flee its hunter, her heartbeat shaking her whole body.

She had risked the child's safety.

She had looked at the child with such anguish

in her eyes that it was as though she had bared her whole heart.

She was a good-time girl—an easy lay who had no appeal for him.

She was a devoted mother who touched some chord deep within him that overran the settings of his moral criteria of what he found desirable in a woman.

Something frightening was overwhelming her. Everything seemed to be happening in slow motion. The ache in her legs that had become so familiar to her over the last couple of weeks had intensified to such a pitch that it made her want to cry out.

Her heart was thudding so much it frightened her. She desperately wanted to sit—no, to lie down, Julie corrected herself tiredly, even as her fingers curled round the metal handrail, so that she could pull herself up the final few stairs and follow Rocco into the villa.

Normally she would have been entranced by the hallway, with its frescoes and its magnificent return staircase to the upper floors, its walls filled with paintings which Julie suspected were each worth a prince's ransom. Normally she would have been thrilled by the opportunity to enjoy such a feast of artworks. But right now she longed so much to lie down that she couldn't think of anything else. She was actually grateful that Rocco was holding Josh.

Rocco was talking to a plump woman whose dark hair was streaked with grey, and who Julie assumed from her demeanour must be the house-keeper. He was handing Josh over to her and she was beaming down at him.

Rocco was turning back to her.

'A room has been prepared for you,' he told Julie. 'Maria will show you to it.'

Julie nodded her head and made to follow Maria, who was already walking up the stairs.

Rocco frowned as he watched Julie. Her face was bone-white and she was staring at the stairs as though she was terrified of them. She took a step towards them—and then stopped moving, suddenly crumpling to the floor.

Rocco covered the distance between them in three easy strides, catching Julie as she collapsed. She wasn't, as he had first thought, unconscious. Her eyes were open and dark with confusion.

'I'm all right. Just a bit tired, that's all.'

Her face looked as bloodless as the marble steps, and he could feel the frantic tolling thud of her heartbeat through the silk blouse where her trenchcoat had fallen open. She was so slight that carrying her felt like carrying a child—except no child had such magnificent breasts. The sensation of them pressed against his own body as he carried her up the stairs stirred his body as well as his senses.

Rocco headed for the stairs still carrying her, ignoring her frantic demands to be put down, simply telling her tersely, 'Keep still.'

Through her embarrassment and her exhaustion Julie had a dizzy impression of white marble stairs, ancestral portraits, a long corridor with white walls, and very dark polished and carved wooden doors—one of which was open.

It was heaven to be lying down, even if her heart was pounding so uncomfortably that it was making her feel sick and anxious.

The bed on which she was lying was large and canopied, in a room that looked as though it had come out of an eighteenth-century film set. A fire burned in the marble fireplace beyond the bed, and Maria was placing Josh in what looked like a brand-new cot at the bottom of the bed, fussing over him. Julie wanted to go to him, but she simply felt too weak.

Rocco frowned as he watched her, folding his arms across his chest and leaning back against the wall. Something was wrong—and, given her lifestyle, it could be drugs. He knew the signs; after all they were easy enough to recognise in these modern times. But, no—this was something other than substance abuse. She was very thin—dieting, then? She hadn't eaten during the flight, and if celebrities were anything to go by it was the fashion to be skeletally thin—skeletally thin but with such large surgically enhanced breasts that women turned themselves into something close to physical freakery.

Maria spoke to him, telling him that the baby was asleep.

Nodding his head, he turned back to the bed and demanded curtly, 'When was the last time you ate a proper meal?'

Julie tried to think, but even that was too much for her. What was the truth? Did she even know? Could she remember? Did she care?

These last weeks had been a nightmare jumble

of trying to look after Josh whilst worrying about Judy's debts. Making a meal for herself had been the last thing on her mind, even if she had had the money to buy proper food. And she hadn't really felt like eating. She had lost James. Not just once, but a second time. Losing him to Judy had hurt dreadfully, but losing him to death had brought another kind of pain—this time not just for herself but for Josh, and for James himself as well. Just the thought of the physical effort it would take to eat had made her feel even worse. She simply had not had the energy.

Her tormentor was still looking at her. Waiting for her to reply. He wouldn't leave her in peace to sleep as she so longed to do until she had answered him. She knew that.

She struggled to sit up.

'I would have had a meal at home in my own flat this evening if I hadn't been virtually hijacked,' she told him, trying to inject a note of scathing contempt into her voice and wondering if it sounded as thin and frail to him as it did to her.

'And before that—at lunchtime, for instance? You ate then? What?'

He was asking her too many questions and too fast.

'There wasn't time. The shop was busy, and Jenny the other girl didn't come in.'

'No lunch, then—breakfast?'

'I had coffee and toast.'

It was a lie. She had *made* coffee and toast, but all she had had time for was a few sips of the coffee before she'd had to take Josh to nursery.

'And every day is like that, is it? You deliberately starve yourself, out of some pathetic belief that being thin makes you more desirable to men like my late brother?'

'No!'

There was real denial as well as outrage in her voice.

'You say no, but it is obvious that you do not eat.'

Spirit flashed in her eyes as she told him fiercely, 'We aren't all rich enough to own private jets and have staff to cook for us, you know.'

Ignoring her attack, Rocco said flatly, 'If you are not starving yourself out of some self-destructive desire to attract the attention of men who can only be aroused by women who look like children and behave like whores, then why are you not more aware of your responsibility to your child? He is wholly dependent on you. After all he has no one else.'

'Do you think I don't know that?' Julie demanded, goaded beyond endurance. 'Do you think I don't think about that every waking hour?' Her eyes were burning with the emotion spilling through her. 'Do you think I don't wish more than anything else that his father were still alive? That he was here to care for and protect his son as I know he would?'

'Antonio?' Rocco eased his shoulders away from the wall on which he had been leaning. He didn't want to admit her championing of his half-brother had hit a nerve that was more sensitive than he had known, causing pain to strike searingly into him. His dead half-brother didn't deserve such loyalty, and she was a fool for giving it to a man who was so unworthy of it.

'The only person my half-brother would ever protect is himself—and if you don't know that then you didn't know him very well.' His voice was harsh and unkind, its contempt making Julie wince as he added, 'But then of course you did *not* know him, did you? How long does it take, after all, to perform the act that created your child? Five minutes? He couldn't even remember your—'

Just in time Rocco caught himself back. It went against his own pride to tell her that Antonio hadn't even been able to remember her name.

Thank goodness he had interrupted her when he had, Julie thought sickly. Otherwise she would have said James's name. She had been so caught up in her grief, but she couldn't do that—not until she had some kind of assurance from Rocco that they would be returned safely to London.

'Dr Vittorio, our family doctor, is coming tomorrow morning to take swabs from the child for DNA testing. Whilst he is here I shall ask him to take a look at you.'

'There is nothing wrong with me.'

The dark eyebrows slanted in ironic query. 'You cannot climb a dozen stone steps without collapsing and you say there is nothing wrong with you? I beg to differ. Did you stay in touch with Antonio when you returned to England?'

The question was casual enough, but it made Julie's heart bound in fear.

What exactly had Judy said about Antonio?

Julie wondered frantically, trying to remember. Her sister had implied that she had told Antonio she was expecting Josh and he had not wanted to know. That was when she had decided to tell James that the baby she was carrying was his.

'I informed him that I was carrying Josh, yes,' Julie lied. 'But he didn't want to know.' That at least was the truth.

'And yet you have just claimed to me that he would have wanted to love and protect his child?'

'As its father, I would hope he would have wanted to do that,' she felt forced to say—even though the truth was that she had been talking about James, who had loved Josh so much, not Antonio.

'As I have already told you, if the child turns out not to be my brother's then you will be compensated for your time and the disruption caused to your life. You will be asked to sign a confidentially agreement never to discuss the matter with anyone—for which you will be paid.'

Julie nodded her head, fighting back her natural instinct to say that she did not want any money. The appropriate time to announce that would be once the DNA results were known.

'And that is all?' she pressed him. 'There is nothing else? No further conditions?'

Rocco walked over to the bed and looked down at her.

'If by that you are daring to imply that I or my brothers would want some kind of sexual payment from you, then let me tell you—'

A sudden wail from the cot had them both looking over to it.

'Now look what you've done,' Julie protested tiredly. 'You've woken Josh.'

'Stay where you are. Maria will attend to him.'

'No. He's my child.'

She was sliding her feet onto the floor, but Rocco was standing in front of her.

'You are in no condition to look after him. Do you really want to risk dropping him again?'

It was a low blow, and it hurt, but to her relief Josh stopped crying and seemed to have gone back off to sleep.

Sleep. How she craved it herself right now.

'It's four o'clock. I suggest you try and get some sleep. Dr Vittorio will be here at ten to do the DNA tests. And, in answer to your question, no—there are no other conditions. All my brothers and I wish to do is fulfil our promise to our father to find Antonio's child—if indeed such a child exists, and was not merely a figment of Antonio's imagination. He was always very good at telling our father what he wanted to hear.'

Long after Rocco had gone Julie lay awake, staring up at the tented silk ceiling of her vast bed, her head aching with too many conflicting thoughts.

Family. What an emotive concept that was. She had always known that their parents preferred Judy, their firstborn, the clever, pretty and bright one, and that she had come a poor second in their affections. Not that they had ever been unkind to her. They hadn't been like that. It was just that they had never been able to hide their joy and delight in Judy, or their mere tolerance of her.

She had craved the closeness of a loving family all through her childhood and her teenage years. She had thought she had found it with James, whom she had met during her time at university.

She had fallen in love with him, and she had loved his parents too, when he had taken her home with him to Newcastle to meet them. But then James had met Judy, and she had known immediately what was happening. Though the man Judy had stolen so easily had clearly not been dear to her, as she had cheated on James early into their relationship.

Judy had betrayed them both, but at least Julie still had Josh.

Had Judy and James and their parents lived Josh would have had a family—parents and grandparents, and a loving auntie in her—but they had not, and now all he had was her.

If he should prove to be Antonio Leopardi's child then he would still have a large extended family, with uncles, aunts and cousins, and of course his grandfather.

Lying sleepless in the dark, Julie acknowledged that for Josh's sake she should hope that he *was* a Leopardi.

CHAPTER FIVE

'WELL, although it can't be confirmed, of course, until I have the results of the blood tests, I am reasonably confident from what you have told me that the cause of your current symptoms is a shortage of iron.'

Dr Vittorio's diagnosis was delivered as he deftly released Julie's arm from the pressure of the cuff he had put round it whilst he took blood samples from her. It left Julie feeling extremely relieved, but even more of a fraud than she had done before.

Her intention to be up early to prove to Rocco how competent and capable she was had been well and truly sabotaged when she overslept, waking only when Maria had arrived carrying a tray containing a formidably hearty breakfast and wearing an equally formidable expression. What was worse was that she had made it clear that she intended to stand over Julie until every last scrap of food had been eaten.

Julie could sense that Maria did not approve of her—and who could blame her, given what she must believe about her? To Maria she was a young woman who slept around and who didn't even know who the father of her child really was.

However much Maria might disapprove of her, though, Julie could not fault her care of Josh.

Julie had been halfway through the poached eggs when Josh had woken up and started to cry, but before she had even had the chance to put down her knife and fork Maria had swung into action.

By the time Julie had finished her breakfast Maria had, under Julie's anxiously protective watch, changed, fed, bathed and dressed Josh, whilst explaining in her hesitant English that she was a mother of five children, a grandmother of twelve and a great-grandmother of three. Julie was a convert to the efficacy of her maternal skills, and ready to do virtually anything to acquire Maria's ability to soothe a fractious baby. Even more importantly and impressively, Maria had also managed to get Josh to feed steadily and happily.

'It is because the little one know that *I* know what is right,' Maria had told Julie firmly, when honesty had obliged Julie to confess how much she worried about Josh's refusal to take all his feed.

'He puts up the fuss because he is scared—because he knows that you are scared,' Maria had unbent enough to tell her.

'I just want to do what's best for him,' Julie had responded emotionally, so relieved to see Josh take all his bottle that she forgot that Maria's loyalties would lie with Rocco Leopardi. 'I love him so much.'

Maria's watchful expression had softened a little then, and she had shaken her head, telling Julie calmly, 'He knows that you love him. And he loves you. He watches for you all the time.'

They had exchanged tentative and cautious smiles, their relationship now on a shared footing of wanting to do their best for Josh.

What with wanting to make the most of the unexpected opportunity to get some valuable baby-raising tips from an expert, and the pleasure of watching Josh lying kicking and gurgling happily on his changing mat—a totally different baby from the fretful child she was used to—

Julie hadn't realised what time it was until Maria had reminded her, pointing out that the doctor would soon be arriving.

Realising that she only had half an hour to shower and dress, Julie had nodded her head gratefully when Maria had offered to take charge of Josh and take him downstairs with her so that Julie could get ready speedily.

Dr Vittorio had been shown up to her room at ten on the dot by Rocco, who had introduced them and then said that Maria would bring Josh back upstairs for his DNA test once the doctor had let Rocco know that he was ready.

When Rocco had described Dr Vittorio as their family doctor Julie had anticipated that he would be an older man, not someone who at the most was only in his very early thirties, a similar age to Rocco himself, although thankfully with a very different and kinder personality.

His kindness and his excellent English had put her completely at her ease.

So much so, in fact, that now that he had given her his early diagnosis of the cause of her symptoms she was able to shake her head and marvel in relief, 'Is that all? I felt so dreadful that I was beginning to worry it could be something serious.'

'Anaemia *is* serious,' Dr Vittorio told her firmly. 'Rocco tells me that you have not been eating?'

'He has only known me a matter of hours, so how he can think he has the right to make that kind of assumption about me?' Julie began heatedly—only to stop self-consciously when she remembered that Dr Vittorio was the Leopardi family's doctor, and that meant his allegiance would be to them, and with it his sympathy.

'You are a single mother with a young child. For Rocco that alone would be enough to bring to the fore his most protective instincts.'

The doctor was speaking as easily and openly as though what he had just said was the most acceptable comment in the world—so much so that Julie wondered if she might have misheard him.

But, as though he sensed her confusion, the doctor continued, 'The death of the Princess shortly after Rocco's birth affected all three of her sons, naturally, but especially Rocco. I can understand that you will feel that his concern is overly protective, and perhaps even an unwarranted interference,' he acknowledged, 'but the death of their mother has left its mark on all her sons.'

'Yes, of course,' Julie was forced to agree, swallowing against her own unwanted sympathy as she added, 'I hadn't realised that that was the case.'

The doctor gave a small, dismissive shrug.

'There was perhaps no reason for Antonio to tell you. He was not, after all, close to his older brothers.'

In those few short words the doctor's contempt and dislike of the dead man was made quite plain.

'As for your anaemia, it is not unusual for a new mother to suffer from such a condition. The child was delivered several weeks short of full term, I understand?'

'Yes,' Julie agreed. 'He was. He was delivered by Caesarean section.'

James had pleaded with Judy not to go ahead with the early Caesarean she had insisted she wanted, having claimed that 'everyone' had their baby a month early to avoid putting on too much weight, but she had refused to change her mind.

'There were complications?'

Julie was getting into deep and dangerous waters now.

'No, not really,' Julie made herself admit.

'So it was more a matter of convenience?' The doctor made it clear that he disapproved with his small frown. 'Such a major operation can affect the health of both mother and child, but I shall know more once I have the results of the blood tests.'

Dr Vittorio had been thorough; Julie had to give him that. He had taken enough blood from her to fill several small phials, taking swabs from inside her mouth as well—presumably because she had told him that she had had a heavy cold.

He had been professional and courteous, apart from that brief lapse when she had admitted that Josh had been delivered in a non-medically necessary pre-full-term Caesarean. He had to know, of course, that she was not sure if Antonio was the father or not, and that must colour his view of her even if he hadn't shown it.

Unlike Rocco Leopardi, who *had* made it very plain what he thought of her morals—or rather what he assumed was the lack of them.

Was she being selfish in hoping that Josh would *not* turn out to be Antonio Leopardi's child? No matter who had fathered Josh, she would still love him every bit as much as she did now, but for James's sake she so much hoped that he was Josh's father, and that in that way a little of him would live on in Josh. James had been such a kind, loving person, with so much to give. Even though he had fallen so desperately in love with Judy he had always been kind and caring towards her, Julie, never wanting to hurt her. But he *had* hurt her.

Julie didn't want to think about that. It was easier and safer to focus on the anger Rocco aroused in her rather than the pain James had caused her. She could never imagine someone like Rocco Leopardi being so gentle with an unwanted ex-lover. He would have no compassion for a woman he no longer wanted in his bed or in his life, and yet when he did desire a woman Julie sensed that his desire would burn white-hot, driven by the kind of sensual sexuality that was still a mystery to her. But then she wasn't really the kind of woman who ignited that kind of desire in a man, was she? She and James had been friends—good pals, who had enjoyed one another's company, whose friendship had grown into love. With James Julie had felt safe from the awkwardness and the dread of mockery and re-

jection she had experienced so much growing up
in Judy's shadow.

During their teens she had had to learn to
accept that boys wanted Judy and found her desirable, and that she paled in comparison—just
as she had had to learn to put a brave smile on
her face when Judy had mocked her publicly in
front of those boys for her lack of allure and
sexual experience.

When she had gone to university and Judy had
gone to train as a beautician Julie had carried
with her the hang-ups of her teens. Julie had met
James when she'd started a postgraduate course.
He had been doing the same course, but had been
a year ahead of her—twenty-four to her twenty-
two. He had laughed gently at her when she had
explained self-consciously and uncomfortably
to him that she was still a virgin and why.

Their lovemaking had been tender and caring,
but somehow Julie had always felt conscious of
trying not to overwhelm James with her own passionate need. She wondered now if that might
have been because she had sensed deep down
inside herself that, despite the fact that he had
said that he loved her, his love had been more the

feelings of a friend than a lover? Because she had feared even whilst she was in his arms that somehow she was not good enough, not worthy of a man's real passion?

If James hadn't felt passionate about her then a man like Rocco certainly wasn't going to be, was he?

Julie was aghast at the speed with which her mind had summoned up such an inappropriate question. Why on earth should she want Rocco to desire her? She didn't. Not at all—not even one tiny little bit. The very thought of being in his arms and his bed made her feel… Julie could feel her face starting to burn as she fought to reject exactly what it did make her feel.

She couldn't imagine Judy feeling humiliated because a stunningly handsome and obviously sensual and sexually experienced man had seen her naked. Far from it. Her late sister would have been the first to take advantage of that kind of situation—she'd have been posing and preening and generally making sure that Rocco was so turned on by her body that he couldn't resist her. Judy had been wholly confident about her own sexuality. Her attitude had been that men found her irresistible. They always had and they always would.

Sometimes Julie wished she could have a little of her sister's self-confidence, although she shrank from the thought of sleeping around in the way that Judy had done. It would have been good, though, to be able to put Rocco in his place by knowing that she had the power to ensure that if she wanted to do so she could make him want her. Not that she would have wanted that, of course. The mere thought of being in bed with a man like him, who could probably do things to a woman's senses with just the touch of his hands on her naked flesh that she couldn't even imagine, was enough to have her heart thudding in wary warning.

To her shock, Julie realised how far her thoughts had strayed from thinking how much she hoped that Josh was James's son.

One thing she was determined on, though, no matter who had fathered Josh. She was his legal guardian and she was not going to give him up—to anyone.

'What will I have to do, if I am anaemic?' she asked the doctor, seeing that he had finished putting everything back in his bag.

'That will depend on how severe your anaemia is. You will certainly need iron tablets, and I think perhaps some of our good warm Sicilian sunshine might do you some good—although you will have to wait a week or so longer for that. Shall I tell Rocco that I am ready to test the little one now, with your agreement?'

Julie nodded her head, watching him as he walked over to the door and then opened it, disappearing through it only to return within a matter of minutes, accompanied by Maria, who was carrying Josh, and Rocco.

Josh was wide awake, his face breaking into a wide smile the minute he saw her.

Julie's heart melted with love.

'He is still a bit underweight,' she told the doctor defensively as she thanked Maria and took Josh from her.

She'd already told him about Josh's post-birth health problems.

The doctor nodded his head, but he was concentrating on checking Josh over.

'He is a little small for his age,' he agreed, before asking Julie to hold Josh whilst he did the DNA test.

A few seconds later, watching as he swabbed the inside of the baby's mouth, Julie's heart gave an uncomfortable little thud.

That was how you took a sample for a DNA test? Had the reason he had swabbed the inside of her mouth been because he intended to test *her* DNA? That he might do so had never occurred to her. What did it matter if he did? she asked herself. She and Josh were related, after all.

Related, yes, but she was not Josh's mother. How accurate would the DNA test be? She didn't dare ask. But Rocco, it seemed, did.

'How accurate an indication of the child's paternity will this test be, and when will we have the results of it?' he asked the doctor.

'It will be accurate enough to make it clear whether or not Antonio is the little one's father,' Dr Vittorio answered him, smiling at Julie and thanking her for holding Josh steady for him. 'And I should have the results through within a week.'

Julie couldn't, of course, ask if he was testing her, and if it was possible to establish her relationship to Josh from the swabs he had taken. They would be suspicious if she did. And besides it didn't matter anyway, did it? She was Josh's legal guardian. But Rocco thought that she was Josh's mother, and she wasn't.

So what? It wasn't her fault that Rocco had got things wrong, was it?

She could have and perhaps should have told him the truth in London.

The Leopardi family were obviously used to getting their own way and making their own rules. If Josh *was* Antonio Leopardi's son then it might suit the Leopardis merely to have Josh's legal guardian to deal with and not his birth mother. Instinctively Julie knew that if Josh was Antonio's son then the Leopardis would do everything in their power to bring him up as one of their own, despite Rocco's assurance to her that he and his brothers considered the mother and baby bond sacrosanct. After all, she was not Josh's mother.

The doctor, Rocco and Maria had all gone, and Julie was free to put Josh down on the beautiful baby mat she had found, along with all the other expensive baby equipment, in the room off her own bedroom which had been fitted out as a nursery.

Josh loved lying on his back, and having the freedom to kick and wave his arms in a room warm enough to allow him to do so in comfort. Julie kissed his bare tummy, and laughed when he tightened his fingers in her hair, gently releasing thcm. He was smiling up at her so happily. Emotional tears filled her eyes. He *was* James's child. She was sure of it.

'You re so precious—do you know that?' she told him, adding softly, 'And your daddy would have loved you so very much.'

'Whoever his daddy actually was.'

Julie's heart lurched and rolled into her chest wall with a crash that seized her breath.

She hadn't realised that Rocco had come back, and that he was now standing in the doorway between the nursery and her bedroom. His voice was as hard as diamonds on glass, and able to penetrate her defences just as easily.

'You may think that I want your half-brother to be Josh's father because your family is rich, but the truth is that I hope he isn't,' she retaliated fiercely, as soon as she could speak.

'Liar. If that was the truth then you wouldn't have made contact with Antonio to tell him that you were pregnant, and you certainly wouldn't have accepted £25,000 from him to buy you off. There's no point in denying it. The cheque went through Antonio's bank account.'

Judy had taken money from Antonio Leopardi? She had never said anything about that to Julie. But then that was typical of Judy, and she would have known how much Julie would have disapproved. All Judy had told her was that Antonio Leopardi didn't want to know that she was pregnant, and that she intended to tell James that the baby was his, having broken off their engagement just before she had gone to Cannes, but knowing that James adored her and would take her back. Which of course he had.

'Strange and extremely clever, the way you've reinvented yourself as such an adoring mother— ready to go without herself in order to benefit her precious child.'

'There's more to being a good mother than buying expensive baby clothes,' Julie defended herself.

'Yes, and the first of those things is knowing who your baby's father is. Unless, of course, you do know but you are keeping quiet about it in the hope of getting more money. If that's the case let me warn you that you're wasting your time. I've already told you what the terms of any deal will be for any child proved not to be Antonio's.'

'How typical of a man like you that you think of everything in terms of money. What I want for Josh can't be bought.'

'A man like me?'

He had left the doorway now and was striding towards her like some dark avenging Lucifer, intent on her destruction. Julie scrambled to her feet to stand protectively in front of Josh.

'You, of course, are an expert on the male sex, aren't you? So tell me. What exactly *is* a man like me?'

He was standing too close to her. Far too close to her.

'You're arrogant and…and selfish. You think that all that matters is what you want, and that just because you want—'

'Just because I want what? You? Is that what you think?'

Julie was horrified. How on earth had the situation got so out of control so quickly?

'No, of course not,' she denied. The way he

was looking at her and the silence he was maintaining unnerved her, and so fatally she rushed into it, adding frantically, 'Why should you want me? I—'

'You what? You want me to want you? You want me to tell you that every centimetre of you is now committed to my memory and engraved on my sexual responses? That in future I shall never be able to look at or touch any woman without comparing her to you? That from now on the pattern of woman carved on my desire is your image? Is that what you want?'

Without waiting for her response—which was just as well, Julie acknowledged inwardly, because she was in no state to think or say anything after hearing what he had just said—he continued dryly, 'Of course such things come at a price, don't they? And for that price I am sure that you would be very willing to assuage my longings and help me expunge those images. We are not, after all, talking of anything here other than a very basic form of lust.'

His voice was soft and mocking, and yet underscored with something age-old, man to woman, that was recognised deep within her. Recognised and responded to, Julie admitted apprehensively. She wanted to run from him, from the unwanted senses deep within her that he had aroused. But—dangerously—even more she wanted to stay. She abhorred what he was saying, and yet a wild, wilful *something* deep inside her wanted, if only for once, to be the kind of woman who would respond easily to such a challenge and enjoy arousing and sharing his lust—who would feel triumph in having aroused it and who would satisfy it and then walk away from it and from him without a single second of guilt or regret.

Very few women walked away from a man like this one, Julie suspected. It would be very empowering to be a woman who could do so. Judy could have done so, of course—but would she have? Would any woman if she thought— If she thought what? That she could tame Rocco and keep him?

What kind of foolish thoughts were those? In Rocco's eyes wasn't she already that woman she had just been describing mentally to herself, since he believed that she was her sister? What would it be like for once in her life to live that role? To know the power of being a woman who gloried in her sexuality and who used it to get whatever she wanted. What would it be like to walk that other road, live that other life, and know her sexuality?

Was she mad? She had other far more important things to think about than finding her own sad, repressed sensuality. She had Josh to think about and to protect.

Rocco gave her a heavy-lidded look of slanting sensuality that heated her blood, spreading arousal through her body unstoppably, like a swift flood-tide flowing swiftly under the drag of a full moon. Inescapable and undeniable, it took her and possessed her, running wild and free within her.

'Nothing to say?' he challenged her.

It would be his fault if she took up his challenge. And he owed her something, didn't he, after the way he had behaved towards her? Why didn't she just take what she wanted? Her heart thumped unsteadily with the enormity of her own unfamiliar thoughts. What she wanted? She didn't want him, did she? No, of course not. But there *was* a temptation there—a fierce, yearning surge as volcanic as Etna itself, demanding expression. Maybe so. But it could not be allowed that expression, Julie warned herself sternly.

What she was thinking was far too dangerous, and a form of madness. Perhaps it was a symptom of her anaemia, she thought shakily, like the weakness in her legs and the pounding in her heart.

'No, I have nothing to say,' she answered him. 'You are not Antonio, after all.'

What on earth had she said *that* for?

'No, I damned well am not.'

The quietly savage words told her all she needed to know about the extent of her folly—and her danger.

She tried to sidestep it—and him—but it was too late. He caught her as easily as he had lifted and carried her the previous night, his hands curling round her upper arms, making it impossible for her to escape.

'You might think you are being very clever, taunting me, but I promise you that I shall extract full payment.' His voice was harsh against her skin, grazing its sensitivity with needle-sharp darts of warning.

'Fine—but you'll have to extract it via your insults, because you won't be getting it any other way,' Julie responded promptly, trying to make her voice sound far more determined and self-confident than she felt.

'No?' The heavy golden leopard's eyes focused on their prey—her.

This had gone too far. What had started out simply as an intention to underline his contempt for Julie had somehow or other twisted and then turned itself around, so that his own weapon was now hurtling back towards him, Rocco admitted grimly. The words he had intended to use to distance himself from her had actually rebounded on him, conjuring up images of her inside his head that were now making him ache with an extremely inconvenient and an even more unacceptable desire.

How could he want a woman like this one? It should have been impossible, based on her sexual morals alone, and doubly so given the fact that he knew she had been one of Antonio's playthings. It should have been impossible, but it wasn't. The sight of her crouched on the floor, her face alight with love as she kissed her baby, had pierced the defences he had thought impenetrable, forcing him into direct contact with his own feelings about the loss of his mother. That in turn had filled him with anger—against himself for being vulnerable, and against her for causing that vulnerability—and now that anger had burned itself into a fierce male desire that was raging out of control inside him.

For his own emotional safety he needed to separate her inside his head from that unwanted image he now had of her as a devoted mother. And the best way to do that was to let his body fill his head with some very different images of her. That was the only reason he wanted her. Out of self-protection. Nothing more.

When he kissed her and she responded to him as he knew she would his brain would register *exactly* what she was. He looked at her mouth and felt her tremble in sensual awareness of his intent. Beneath the silk blouse she was wearing—the blouse he had paid for, like all the other expensive clothes now hanging up in the room's wardrobes—he could see quite clearly not just the tight thrust of her nipples but also the faint raised edge that marked the place where the areolae of her breasts rose from the surrounding flesh. Almost absently he removed his right hand from her arm and slowly traced the raised line.

Julie shuddered violently, and closed her eyes in shocked awareness of how deep the abyss of her own sexuality actually was—and how dangerous. If a simple touch like this one could have such an effect on her, then what would his kiss do to her? How far would it take her down into the hot velvet darkness of that place she had never been? She felt dizzy and light-headed—with longing? With lust? Because she was anaemic? Did it matter why? Wasn't it only important that somehow she didn't want to resist what she was feeling, that she wanted to bring it and the man who was the cause of it closer instead of pushing them away?

His touch on her nipple, stroking it between his thumb and forefinger, shot pangs of erotic sensation deep into her. She looked up at his mouth, so beautifully carved that it could have been painted by a Renaissance artist, indenting at the corners, his bottom lip sensually full. Once against her own mouth it was both a possession and a caress, drawing her deeper under the spell of her own sexuality. She could feel his breath—warm, scented with maleness—as he urged her closer, and the hand that had been holding her arm pressed flat into the arch of her spine, so that her body fitted itself to his. Weakly she leaned into him, savouring the sensation of his hand on her breast, her own weight against his thighs, soft flesh against hard muscle, the one accommodating the other, her softness excited by that accommodation of his hardness and wanting to take things further.

Here in this unknown place where she now was there was no need for her to watch or regulate her reactions, no need for her to care how she might be judged, or to feel humbled as she had done with James—grateful for his love, knowing that his passion did not match her own, and desperate not to do anything that would tip the balance of his acceptance into male revulsion of too much female sexual need.

Here she could step away from the image her life had moulded her into and find out what it was like to be free to truly be herself. Softly the siren song of her own desire whispered its addictive message of persuasion to her.

His mouth was skilled and knowing. This was sexuality stripped bare, raw and urgent, binding her to its will and her own need. His tongue probed the seal of her closed lips, his hand kneading her breast, so that the twin assault on her senses made her body ache in time to his rhythm. She could hear the sound of her own breathing in all its ragged and charged betrayal of her need. She melted into him—and then tensed as she heard Josh cry.

Immediately she snapped back to reality, ignoring Rocco as he released her to let her go to Josh.

If there had been a moment when they had looked at one another, sharing regret, then she did not want to think about it.

'I have some business matters to attend to. If there is anything you need for the child, please inform Maria.'

Julie kept her back to Rocco, nodding her head to signify that she had heard him, not daring to so much as breathe properly, never mind turn round, until she was sure he had left the room.

Her hands trembled as she held Josh. She was icy-cold with reaction to her own behaviour. What on earth had possessed her? The emotions and feelings she had experienced had been so frighteningly alien to everything that she felt about herself.

Or had they? Had they instead been a reflection of the anger that had been locked inside her for so long? Because the reality Julie admitted was that she had been angry for a very long time: angry with Judy, angry with herself, even angry with James. So much so that the anger Rocco Leopardi had made her feel had been the burning spark that had ignited a positive volcano of emotion.

Well, she had certainly confirmed his opinion of her as someone little better than a call girl, Julie acknowledged shakily as she dressed Josh. A wanton hussy who had offered herself to him. A wanton hussy who didn't have the first idea of what it was like to truly experience sexual passion—who had, in fact, subdued her longing to do so with the only lover she had known.

It was just as well Rocco didn't really want her. If he had made love to her he might just have fired her passion to the extent that her desire for him would have burned out of control.

What would it be like to really be wanted by a man like Rocco? To be desired by him, to be taken to his bed and kept there until he had aroused and then slaked their mutual passion past the point where either of them was in control of themselves or their destinies? How dangerous it would be to crave that kind of intimate possession from a man like him. How much safer she had been walking the path she had, where her desires and her emotions had been closeted and controlled.

CHAPTER SIX

IT WAS three days now since she had arrived on Sicily, and finally the wind had dropped and it had stopped raining.

This morning for the first time Julie had woken up to blue skies, with the dazzling beauty of a snow-capped Etna visible for once without its veil of mist and rain.

Sicily's weather like Sicily's history, was turbulent and demanding, Julie had learned, and now its passion was softened in the aftermath of its own excess, as if sated by the demands it had made at the height of its need to prove itself.

Whilst Josh had napped she had walked slowly through the formal salons of the *piano nobile*, gazing with awe at their magnificence. The most homely—if such a word could be used to describe such wonderful rooms—was the Sala degli Arazzi, with its priceless tapestries, from which a set of double doors opened out into the library, with row upon row of leather-bound volumes and silk curtains woven, so Maria had told her, in Lyons, to a design that had later been destroyed so that no one else could ever use it.

The rooms led one into the other in the classic *enfilade* style of the eighteenth century—the library giving way to the Chinese Salon, with its lacquered furniture, and then the Egyptian hallway, rectangular and galleried, with niches housing marble busts. Beyond that was a large square room with late eighteenth-century alle- gorical frescoes and elegant gilt wood furniture, its chairs and sofas covered in a blue silk that had also been specially woven in Lyons.

The last room overlooked an inner courtyard garden dominated by a large baroque fountain ornamented with mythical creatures spouting water into the stone pool beneath it. And yet for all its magnificence the house still had the definite air of being a home. Fresh flowers in ornate priceless bowls set on equally priceless furniture, filled the air with their scent, and Maria orchestrated her own army of skilled workers to keep the house clean.

Now, Julie made her way downstairs to the kitchen.

Through the open door she could smell the scent of citrus for the first time, wafting into the courtyard on the soft caress of a breeze from the orange and lemon groves that lay beyond the villa.

'You have taken your medicine?' Maria demanded.

Julie smiled and nodded her head. She had been taking iron tablets twice a day for the last two days, on the instructions of Dr Vittorio, who had said he wanted her to take them pending the results of her blood tests. She had to admit that already she was feeling more like her old self.

Julie had grown used to the older woman's sharpness now, and even if Maria disapproved of her, Julie had to admit that when it came to Josh, Maria was as dotingly protective as though he were a part of her own family.

'It is just as well that Rocco is a strong man as well as a good one. It will be hard for him to watch the little one.'

'Because he could be Antonio's son?' Julie queried.

'No. It is seeing you with the child that will be hard for him,' Maria corrected her firmly.

'Why?' Julie asked, her attention more on Josh, who she was feeding, than on Maria who, Julie had learned, enjoyed a good gossip.

'Because he will have to witness the little one enjoying something that he never had. The love and attention of a mother,' Maria announced, looking up from the dough she was kneading.

Julie frowned—it was easy and tempting, if unrealistic, to imagine that Rocco had sprung fully formed and armed into adult male maturity without ever going through any process that involved him being dependent on anyone, much less a mere female.

'The Princess—his mother—died with Rocco's birth,' Maria told Julie dramatically. 'Poor woman. Many said that she did not want to live because of the cruelty of her husband. It was always known that the Prince only married her for her family's land, and the fact that her blood lines went back as far as his. That is the way with the nobility. She was much younger than him—only seventeen when they married— and convent-reared. Poor girl, she fell in love with him at first sight. But he was not the kind of man to be satisfied with a young, innocent wife. Not when there was already another in possession of his heart.'

Maria was certainly relishing the telling of her story, Julie acknowledged ruefully, although it sounded more like a fictitious drama than any kind of reality. She smiled down at Josh, who was sucking strongly on his bottle, feeding so much better than he had been.

'I dare say she might have borne it better if there had been many mistresses and not just the one,' Maria continued. 'And such a one, who refused to know her place,' she added darkly. 'The poor little Princess didn't stand a chance against one such as her, experienced in the ways of keeping a man within her power. She boasted openly to anyone who would listen to her that the Prince loved her and not his wife. There were no tears shed by either of them when the Princess died, I can tell you that, and I dare say if she could Isabella would have seen her children in Princess Lucia's grave with her.

'But the Prince, of course, knew what was due to his blood. The Princess had given him three fine sons, but now she was dead and he was free to marry Isabella. Five years later she had her own son, and the Prince doted on him in the same way that he did on her. No other man could have got away with such shameful behaviour but the Prince answers to no higher authority. The Leopardis are born into pride—they wear it like their skin and cannot be separated from it,' Maria informed her with obvious relish.

Julie frowned. Rocco had not made any mention of Josh having a grandmother, but maybe that was understandable in the circumstances.

'Where is Isabella now?' she asked Maria. Josh had finished his bottle and she lifted him against her shoulder to wind him.

'Ha! She is where she deserves to be—in her grave. She fell on the top steps of the castle tower and broke her neck. Some say that the ghost of the Princess pushed her, and certainly no one apart from the Prince and her son mourned her death. She had no understanding of the way things are, or of what it means to be a Leopardi wife and the mother of Leopardi sons. She was not worthy.'

Maria might gossip about the Leopardi family,

but she was at the same time steadfastly loyal to them, and ready to defend them against anyone who might dare to criticise them, Julie knew.

'It must have been hard for Rocco, growing up without his mother,' she agreed.

'It was hard for all three of them,' Maria told her. 'Their father had no time for them, and Isabella made sure they knew that she held the whip hand—sometimes literally, I can tell you. I worked up at the castle then, and there was more than one occasion when someone would come down from the nursery asking for some of Cook's special salve for Falcon's wounds. Him being the eldest, he always took the punishment for the other two, you see.'

Poor little boys, Julie thought sympathetically. But Rocco wasn't a boy now. He was a man. In an attempt to ignore the ache tightening her lower body, she paced the length of the kitchen, holding Josh against her shoulder.

'I'd like to take Josh outside,' she told Maria. 'Perhaps go for a walk. There's a baby buggy in the nursery.'

'It is too cold,' Maria told her immediately.

'The sun's out,' Julie protested.

'We have a wind here that slices into the flesh like a knife,' she warned Julie. 'On one side of the island even the vines and lemon trees have to be cut close to the ground to protect them from it. Here we might be on the most favoured part of the coast, where the nobility built their fine summer villas so that they could enjoy the summer breeze away from the heat of their estates, but it is still not warm enough for any walking. Besides, you would have to ask Rocco for his permission, and he is not here.'

Immediately Julie could feel herself stiffening in angry resentment at the thought of having to ask Rocco Leopardi's permission for anything. It was bad enough that she had to accept his charity by living under his roof, eating his food, and worst of all wearing the clothes that he had paid for. She was not going to let him control her by forcing her to ask him for permission to do something as ordinary as go for a walk, Julie told herself firmly, instantly and rebelliously making up her mind that taking Josh for a walk was exactly what she was going to do.

It might not have been quite as easy as she had imagined to get the buggy—a solid affair, which was heavier than she had expected—down all the stairs, but Julie possessed an obstinacy that would not allow her to give up. Even though virtually all the good work done by the iron tablets had been undone by the time she had got the buggy down to the ground floor. Her heart was racing and thumping, and the horrible sense of needing to lie down was back, but she wasn't going to give in. She still had to go back upstairs to get Josh after all.

Ten minutes later, as she pushed the buggy along a dirt road towards the grove of citrus trees up ahead of her, Julie admitted that the wind *was* colder than she had expected. Josh, though, at least was securely protected from it, carefully wrapped up in several layers of warm clothes and tucked up securely in the buggy. She was not so fortunate, having come out in one of the fine wool skirts that filled the wardrobes of her bedroom. It was off white, and worn with a beautiful grey Italian knitted top and a pair of butter-soft steel-grey leather shoes with a small heel, but she was without a coat, having been deceived by the sunshine and by the warmth generated from her exertions with the buggy into thinking it was a lot warmer than it actually was. The sun was warm, but the wind, once she had left the protection of the courtyard, cut into her like a knife—just as Maria had predicted that it would.

Only her stubborn determination not to be dictated to any more than she had to be kept her from turning back—that and the fact that Josh was smiling happily, so obviously enjoying the outing that she didn't have the heart to take him back.

She'd only intended to go as far as the citrus grove, but what she hadn't bargained for was the fact that the land sloped down to it, so that once she turned round to come back she had to walk uphill, buffeted by the wind that had now blown clouds up out of nowhere to fill the sky and blot out the sun.

The effort she was having to make to push the heavy buggy along the muddy track should have warmed her up, but strangely it seemed to be having the opposite effect of making her shiver.

She felt the first spot of rain at the same time as she realised she had walked a lot farther than she had thought and was still a good half an hour away from the villa, judging from her current frustratingly slow rate of progress. By the time she had pulled up the hood of the buggy and fastened on the protective waterproof cover it was raining quite hard, and the buggy, which might have travelled at speed on tarmac or proper pavements, was difficult to push on a dirt track that was rapidly turning into muddy puddles.

How could it have gone so cold in such a short space of time? The rain felt like ice, reminding her of London and the cold winter they had just endured, especially now that the storm clouds had grown so heavy that it almost seemed dark. Mount Etna, whose snow-capped summit she had admired only that morning through the windows of the villa, was now wreathed in a mist of ominously grey cloud.

It was too late now to wish that she hadn't given in to that foolish surge of rebellious defiance.

Her head was bent into the wind as she pushed the buggy, whilst her body shivered and her heart pounded with the sick exhaustion that was draining her of energy. And Julie didn't even know that she wasn't alone anymore until she saw the dark male hands on the buggy's handles next to her own.

'Rocco!'

Did Rocco hear the relief in her voice beneath the angry guilt? If he did he wasn't saying so. The look in his eyes as she turned her head to glance uncertainly up at him was one of incensed biting disapproval.

She was trapped between him and the buggy, but the warmth coming off his body felt so blissful that she didn't feel inclined to object.

'Here—put this on,' he told her, thrusting a thick leather jacket over her shoulders. His own jacket, Julie recognized, as she caught the scent of him on it. He didn't wait for her to obey him, but instead pulled the jacket round her and removed one of her hands from the buggy to push it into the sleeve, whilst holding securely on to the buggy himself with his free hand.

'You need this yourself,' Julie protested, realising now that he had turned her to face him that he hadn't brought the jacket with him, but had removed it from his own body.

He shook his head, ignoring her protest. The rain was coming down so heavily now that it had already plastered the fabric of his shirt to his body, revealing the outline of the solidly muscled torso beneath it.

'What is it with you?' he demanded furiously, raising his voice so that it would carry above the increasing noise of the fiercely buffeting wind. 'You claim to love your child, and yet you do something like this—bringing him out here when you were warned that the weather isn't suitable.'

Maria had obviously told him what she had said to her, Julie realised. 'I wanted him to have some fresh air.'

'Did you? He could have had that in the court-yard—in safety.'

'He *is* safe.'

'No thanks to you.'

That was too much.

'I would never put Josh at risk. He's wrapped up and warm.'

'And in your care. And you are suffering from a debilitating illness that doesn't allow you enough strength to climb a flight of stairs without the risk of passing out, never mind go for a walk in these conditions.'

'That's not fair,' Julie protested. 'I've been a lot better since I've been taking the iron tablets.'

'A lot better?' She could hear the derision in his voice. 'I watched you just now—you were so exhausted that you could hardly put one foot in front of the other, never mind anything else. What is it with you British that you have this need to trudge over every landscape even when common sense must tell you that it is inhospitable?'

'I don't know—probably the same level of gene that makes Leopardi men so bossy and arrogant,' Julie was stung into retorting.

All the time he had been hectoring her they had been walking back towards the villa, with Rocco pushing the buggy and making much better progress than she had done as she struggled to keep up with him.

'You claim that you are better,' Rocco told her, ignoring her comment about his arrogance and returning instead to a subject that obviously suited him much better since it involved criticising her, Julie thought darkly as he continued, 'Look at you now. You are struggling to cover a few yards. Don't bother denying it. And what the hell were you about, coming out without a coat?'

'What's wrong?' Julie yelled at him, her self-control snapping. 'Are you worried that I might have ruined the expensive clothes you paid for?'

'Don't be ridiculous. You should know perfectly well that my concern isn't for a few pieces of cloth. Your child is my concern—just as he should be yours. Didn't you stop to think what might happen if you collapsed, or how long the pair of you might be out here? You've seen how the weather has turned. You must be able to feel the force of the wind.'

Julie could only nod her head in grudging admission of the truth of his words.

'If this wind had caught the buggy it could quite easily have turned it over. The pair of you would have been lucky to get away with pneumonia—if fate had been less kind you could have died.'

Rocco wasn't going to tell her just how he had felt when he had come back from a site meeting earlier than he had planned to discover that she and Josh were missing—only to learn from Maria that Julie had been talking about going out for a walk.

Rocco had no idea what had made him check the track that led to the lemon grove first, but she was damned lucky that he had.

He was furiously angry with her for putting at risk all the effort he had gone to to get her and Josh here and thus start to fulfil his part of the responsibility he and his brothers had taken on. A prize fool he would have looked if something had happened to her and the child whilst they were in his care. And if Josh did turn out to be Antonio's child then there was no doubt that his father would have accused him—totally without any foundation or truth—of being only too glad that Josh had not survived.

Rocco could feel his heart thudding with a mixture of anger and relief. Relief that he had found them and anger because he had had to come and do so.

'What the hell did you want to go out for anyway? No, let me guess—you were bored and missing your normal way of life. Well, you won't find the kind of party scene that you like so much, nor the men that go with it, here.'

'I wasn't looking for any party scene or any man,' Julie denied. 'In fact a man is the last thing I want.'

They were back, and she was exhausted. Exhausted and sick with the fear instilled in her by Rocco's far too graphic descriptions of what might have happened to Josh. Despite accepting that she was at fault, somehow she was still so angry at him that her anger was virtually all that was keeping her on her feet.

It was Rocco who now removed Josh, who had miraculously fallen fast asleep and stayed that way, from his buggy, and Rocco who carried him upstairs to the nursery—whilst Julie trailed behind him, willing herself to find the strength to make it to the bedroom. Josh looked so small clasped against Rocco's shoulder—and so safe.

'You'd better take this,' Julie told Rocco ungraciously, removing his jacket and holding it out to him at arm's length as she informed him, 'I'll take Josh.'

'I may as well put him in his cot, since he's asleep.'

He was refusing to give Josh to her? Why? What did he think she was going to do? Drop him?

'He can't go in his cot like that. He's wearing an outdoor all-in-one suit.'

'Yes, but presumably it comes off?'

Rocco wasn't even bothering to wait for her response, or to give her demand even a second's proper consideration. He was ignoring her, just as though she had no say at all in what was best for Josh.

Julie fumed as Rocco carried Josh through into the nursery, leaving her to drop his leather coat onto her bed and hurry after him, protesting, 'There's no need for you to do that. You might wake him up.'

He was still ignoring her, laying Josh on his changing table with unexpected expertise and then efficiently removing his outdoor suit. Josh slept on obliviously.

'Perhaps you'd like to check his nappy and change him as well?' Julie suggested sarcastically.

'What I'd like is to feel that he's got someone in his life who takes a responsible attitude towards his care. But right now, much as I'd like to think that, I can't,' Rocco told her pointedly.

Guilt and pride warred with one another inside Julie's heart. She hated having her care of Josh questioned, but at the same time she was guiltily aware that she *had* allowed herself to be blinded by her own stubborn determination not to let Rocco dictate to her what she could and could not do.

'If anything had happened to Josh I'd never have forgiven myself,' she admitted in a low, tortured voice, her guilt and honesty winning the battle.

Rocco hid his surprise at her admission.

Somehow it was out of character for the kind of woman he knew her to be—and yet, if he was honest, this wasn't the first time in their short acquaintanceship when she had surprised him and challenged his perceptions of her. Nor the first time either that she had driven him to the point where she had tested his self-control way beyond its normal limits, he admitted—and not just the self-control that governed his temper. He was still battling to deny the extent to which she aroused him sexually—and failing, as his body was telling him very clearly right now.

How was it possible for him to want a woman he could only despise? A drowned rat of a woman who ricocheted between stubborn folly, aggressive antagonism and the kind of passionately intense sexual response to him that his head told him had to be manufactured, given her history, but that this body swore was the adult version of being a child let loose in a sweet shop.

Deftly, Rocco slid Josh into his cot and covered him up.

'Maria said to tell you that she's making you a special dish of liver cooked to her special recipe for dinner, along with a good helping of spinach. Or perhaps I should have said *warn* you,' he told Julie dryly.

Maria had taken the doctor's dietary suggestions for Julie to heart, with the result that iron-rich meat and greens had been served to her at every meal since the doctor's visit apart from at breakfast, when she was served her iron in the form of eggs.

Julie managed a wan smile. 'I was hoping to persuade Maria that cannelloni filled with spinach and ricotta cheese would be just as beneficial.'

'You need to get out of those wet clothes.'

'Yes.' Rocco was walking past her and heading for the bedroom door. Julie took a deep breath and told him reluctantly, 'Thank you for…for coming to find us.'

Her head was bowed, so she didn't see the way his gaze rested on her before he said coolly, 'There's no need to thank me. After all, I have a vested interest in protecting Josh.'

He'd gone before Julie had time to raise her head and look at him—much to her relief. The last thing she needed right now was to endure the discomfort of having him realise that his pointed reminder that it was Josh who mattered to him and not her had hurt her. Hurt her? How crazy was that? How could a man she had only known four days possibly be able to hurt her emotionally?

It was possible for one heart to recognise another in the space of a single heartbeat, with all that that meant, she reminded herself. But she and Rocco didn't have hearts that recognised each other, did they? In fact Rocco probably didn't have a heart at all.

No heart? Then what was pumping the blood round that magnificent body?

And it *was* magnificent. The way in which his damp shirt had clung to his flesh had shown her that. Julie rubbed her eyes. She was cold and wet, and in need of a hot shower and probably a rest. A sudden gust of wind drove the rain against her bedroom window, making her shiver as she contemplated what might have so easily happened if Rocco hadn't come to look for them. He might not have said it in so many words, but she knew he thought that she wasn't fit to have charge of Josh, and perhaps he was right. She hadn't done a very good job so far of looking after her little nephew, had she? It was only since he had been here that Josh had finally started to thrive and put on weight.

What was going to happen if he *did* turn out to be Antonio's child?

Did she really need to ask herself that? Rocco and his brothers would take Josh from her. They would find him a proper, suitable substitute mother; they would surround him with all the care that Leopardi money could buy; they would cherish and protect him.

But she would love him, Julie told herself fiercely. And surely that meant something?

CHAPTER SEVEN

THE sight of the buggy, its wheels solid with mud and grit, abandoned in the hallway, acted on Rocco's temper like a match to a highly flammable substance, representing as it did everything about the current state of his life—both professional and private—that infuriated and irked him.

He was in the middle of a building project on which every day of work lost cost money and which the heavy rain of Sicily's always unpredictable pre-spring weather was already threatening to delay; his site manager—a passionate Lombardese whose personal life was more dramatic than anything that had ever been put on at La Scala—had just informed him that he was taking a week's leave because his wife was threatening to leave him over an affair he had been having with an underwear model and he needed to go home to sort things out; somehow his grandfather had got wind of Josh's presence at the villa, and according to Maria there had been five telephone calls from the castle since the morning, commanding Rocco's presence at his father's bedside, and on top of all that a woman who should have meant nothing whatsoever to him at all was disturbing and disrupting his thoughts and emotions as well as his desires, in a way that made him feel furious at his own inability to control what he was experiencing.

And as if all of that wasn't enough, that same woman had had the idiocy to put both herself and her child at risk because she had felt that the baby needed some fresh air. Had she no sense of her own vulnerability? Had she really thought she was well enough to push a buggy up a steep incline over thick mud, when only days ago she had hardly been able to climb a flight of steps? If her child *was* Antonio's son then she would soon learn that his father wouldn't tolerate or make allowances for her stubborn foolishness in the way that Rocco had.

Rocco looked at his watch. He had better drive over to the castle before his father brought on his own end with a self-induced heart attack, he acknowledged grimly.

* * *

Julie looked longingly towards her bed. Josh—
fed, bathed and content—was clearly not suffering any setback from their walk, but she was
exhausted, she admitted, and still cold inside
right through to her bones, despite her shower
and the warm, dry clothes she was now wearing.

It was only half past three—plenty of time for
her to have a rest before dinner.

At least she was over her latest bout of
whatever alien weirdness it was that was taking
her over and somehow convincing her that she
needed to experience the full intimacy of raw,
passionate sex and with Rocco Leopardi, Julie
thought with relief as she lay down on top of
the bed, too exhausted to even think of getting
undressed. It shocked her not just that she could
even feel like that, but also because of the
unwanted and upsetting anger she had discovered within herself—especially against James.
After all, it wasn't his fault that he had not
wanted her as passionately as she had done
him. It would be far safer and make far more
sense for her to simply accept that she was not
the sort of woman to inspire intense sexual
passion in the kind of man she could love.

And that other kind of man? The kind like Rocco Leopardi? That kind of man she did not *want* to love—the kind of man to whom intense sexual passion came as naturally as breathing and meant nothing other than an appetite to satisfy. It simply wasn't possible for her to want to have sex with a man she knew despised her. Her pride and her self-respect would not allow it. And anyway, that had all been a silly mistake brought on by the fact that she hadn't been feeling well. She didn't really want him at all, Julie told herself firmly, before finally allowing herself the luxury of sliding into sleep.

His interview with his father over, Rocco felt the familiar surge of relief that always accompanied his departure from the castle. His father had tried to pressure him into taking Josh to the castle for him to inspect, claiming that he 'would know Antonio's child immediately,' but Rocco had remained steadfast, pointing out that in law it was the DNA test result that would be accepted as prove of parentage, not his grandfather's recognition. Naturally the older man hadn't liked that, and the kind of argument familiar to Rocco from his youth had ensued, during which the Prince had accused all three of his sons from his first marriage of having their own agenda, claiming that they had always resented his second wife and their half-brother.

This had led on to the Prince stating that Rocco and his brothers were deliberately trying to keep his grandson from him, despite having given him their word that they would find him— all of which Rocco had refuted, refusing to allow his father to bully him or, when that failed, use emotional blackmail to force Rocco to bring Josh to the castle.

'I am not yet the powerless old man you think me,' the Prince had told Rocco. 'I still have my friends, and I warn you, Rocco, that no one will keep my Antonio's child from me.'

'No one wants to keep him from you, Father,' Rocco had pointed out. 'But first we have to as-certain if the child is in fact Antonio's.'

'You should let me, his father, be the judge of that. What man does not know his own flesh? No man who dares to call himself a true man,' the Prince had countered theatrically.

It was a pity that his father had found out about

Josh's presence on the island, Rocco admitted, because it could only complicate matters.

The sudden, unplanned surge of power that came from his foot pressing hard on the accelerator of his car warned him of the danger of his antagonistic feelings over the fact that Julie had been Antonio's lover. His *lover*? Rocco's mouth twisted. Since when had the kind of shallow, meaningless sex Antonio had indulged in ever had anything to do with love? He pitied Josh, knowing as he did himself what it did to the soul to know that your life had been created by an act divorced from any kind of emotional communion.

Given her obvious determination to do exactly the opposite of whatever he said to her, even when that meant risking Josh's life, Rocco suspected that he would be wasting his time, having decided he ought to warn Julie that his father might seek to trick her into taking Josh to see him. Nevertheless, his own conscience was insisting that it was something he must do, he acknowledged, as he tapped on her half-open bedroom door before pushing it fully open and going in.

The sight of Julie lying fast asleep and fully

dressed on top of the bed checked him, causing him to frown in a renewal of the fury he had felt when he had first seen her pushing the buggy uphill along the muddy track, looking so frail that she'd seemed almost on the point of collapse.

He had used the Leopardi authority he rarely needed to resort to with Dr Vittorio after the doctor had examined Julie, to find out if he genuinely thought that Julie was merely suffering from a lack of iron or if he suspected that something more serious might be wrong.

At first Luca Vittorio had refused to answer him. But Luca and Rocco had played together as boys. When Rocco had pointed out that he simply wanted to know so that he could ensure Julie received the treatment she needed, Luca had relented and shaken his head, saying that he was fairly sure her symptoms were caused by an iron deficiency, but that that did not mean that it wasn't serious—dependent upon the extent of the deficiency and its cause. The iron tablets Luca had prescribed were a stop-gap solution, designed only to boost her energy levels pending the results of the tests.

Julie knew the situation as well as Rocco did,

and yet she had still risked potentially causing more damage to her health. She infuriated him in ways he had not known existed until she came into his life, Rocco admitted grimly. Just as she— Just as she what? Aroused him in exactly the same intense and extraordinarily all-encompassing way?

She did not arouse him. He was a man. A man who had been living the life of a monk for the better part of a year. And since that was more by accident than design, because of the amount of work he had taken on, it was only natural that when a woman threw herself at him as she had done he was going to respond. The fact that he had even momentarily been tempted by her filled him with self-derision.

The door between the bedroom and the nursery was open, drawing Rocco towards it. How could his father expect anyone to believe that it was possible to 'know' an unknown child's bloodlines? Rocco looked down into the cot, where Josh lay fast asleep. Being here was doing Josh good. He had put on weight, and his skin looked less sallow, warmer.

Rocco leaned closer and studied the sleeping

baby. His fluff of dark hair had a slight curl to it. All the Leopardi men had thick dark hair with a curl, even if in adulthood Rocco had chosen to have his own hair cut so short that its curl couldn't be seen. Josh's eyelashes fanned out across his cheeks. His eyes were growing darker in colour. But what, after all, did that mean? Rocco could see nothing in Josh that reminded him of Antonio, but that would not stop his father from doing so if he was so minded. His father might now be bedridden, and living in the shadow of his own death, but he was still a very powerful and autocratic man—a man who was used to making sure that his will prevailed, no matter what the cost to others.

Rocco could see a difficult future ahead for this child lying so peacefully asleep in his cot if he did turn out to be Antonio's son—and an even harder one for his mother. For all that he would welcome Josh into the family, Rocco knew his father would feel very differently about Josh's mother. The Prince had indulged and spoiled Antonio from the moment he had been born, turning a blind eye to all his excesses as he grew to adulthood. How much had that indulgence been responsible for Antonio's lifestyle and ultimately for his death?

Rocco smoothed the cover over Josh's sleeping body, smiling at the small star-shaped little hand and watching Josh's fingers curl round his own index finger, as though even in sleep the baby instinctively reached for the security of an adult touch.

The first thing Julie saw when she woke up was Rocco, bending over Josh's cot, with one hand on the side of the cot and the other inside it. Her heart lurched into her chest wall. Rocco might deny it, but neither he nor his brothers had any reason to love Josh. They certainly hadn't loved their own half-brother. Maria had gossiped to her, saying that all three brothers were independently wealthy, and there was certainly no question of any child of Antonio's usurping their right to inherit their father's titles. But if their father chose to leave his grandson money they had assumed would be theirs…

Immediately her protective instincts had her on her feet and hurrying into the nursery, demanding sharply, 'What are you doing?'

Rocco turned his head to look at her, but didn't remove his hand.

Protectively, Julie went round to the other side of the cot to look anxiously at Josh, only able to relax when she recognised that he was breathing safely and easily. That should have been enough to steady her, but the sight of Josh's small hand curled tightly round Rocco's finger caused a fresh lurch of her heart—this time from angry pain rather than fear for the little boy.

Rocco had no right to enter the nursery and watch over the child in a way that should have belonged only to Josh's father. Julie had to fight not to snatch Josh up and hold him tightly, but she had to satisfy herself with demanding, 'Why are you in here?'

'Because I choose to be. This is after all my home, and Josh could be my nephew. It's only natural that I should want to check that he hasn't taken any harm from the reckless behaviour of his mother.'

His suave response, with its reminder of things she'd rather forget, increased Julie's anxiety—but that was nothing to the sudden downward plunge of her heart when Rocco gently eased his finger free of Josh's grip and urged Julie back into her own room with a calm, 'I have news.

'Unfortunately my father is aware that you and Josh are on the island,' he began, 'and even more unfortunately he has decided that he will know Antonio's son, without recourse to a DNA test, the minute he sets eyes on him. I realize, of course, that you will probably be delighted by the thought that my father in his desperation to find his grandson may well decide that Josh *is* Antonio's child.'

'Well, that is where you are wrong,' Julie denied immediately. 'Surprising though you might find it, the truth is that I do *not* want Josh to be Antonio's son. I'd much rather that James is his father—after all, James was prepared to marry…me, and bring Josh up as his own.'

The minute the hot words were out Julie wished desperately that she had not said them. But it was too late for those regrets now. Rocco was giving her a very grim look indeed, and as she watched he strode over to her bedroom door and closed it, turning round to confront her.

'So there *is* another man whom you know could be Josh's father?' he demanded coldly.

'Not is—was,' Julie was forced to admit. 'He's dead now. Killed in a rail accident.'

'Why have you not said anything of this before?'

'You hardly gave me the chance. All you cared about was proving whether or not your half-brother was Josh's father.'

'You say you do not want Josh to be Antonio's, and yet you contacted Antonio to tell him that you were having his child. He gave you money to buy you off.'

Rocco was angry—furiously, savagely angry—at the thought of all the time that had been wasted when with a few simple words she could have said right from the start that Antonio was not Josh's father.

'Was there ever any chance that Josh might be Antonio's? Or was it all a scam cooked up between you and your lover to get money out of Antonio for a child that you knew all along was not his? Answer me,' he demanded harshly, 'unless you want me to shake the answer out of you.'

'I don't know,' Julie admitted.

CHAPTER EIGHT

Rocco stared at her.

'You don't know what?' he demanded caustically.

'I don't know who Josh's father was,' she told him truthfully. 'But I do know that I want it to be James and not Antonio.'

'You loved him? This James?'

What was he doing? What possible difference did it make what she had felt, and why should he care?

'Yes.' The tears Julie didn't want to shed blurred her vision and her voice.

'But you still had sex with my brother.'

His voice might be flat, but there was no mistaking the contempt it held.

'James and I had quarrelled. I thought it was over. I went on holiday and…and it just happened…'

'It just happened?' Rocco mimicked her. 'Just like that? A moment of weakness when you were missing the man you really loved. Is that what you mean?'

Julie swallowed. That was what had happened to her when she had for those awful, dreadful minutes actually wanted him, Rocco, wasn't it? The betrayal of her long-standing love for James had merely been a shameful moment of madness and weakness.

'Yes,' she agreed woodenly.

Rocco strode towards her, his hands gripping her shoulders so tightly that his fingers dug painfully into her tender flesh. He half shook her as he told her bitingly, 'Liar. What "just happened", as you call it, was that Antonio hired you—along with another girl—to indulge him in his sexual fantasies. We know that because we found the receipt amongst his papers—although of course you and the other girl who put on that shabby little show for him weren't the only entertainment he paid for during his visit to Cannes. At least the madam he used ensured that her girls had regular health checks—the cost of those was on the bill as well. I must say, though, that I'm surprised you used your real name instead of a fictional name of some kind.'

Rocco made a sound of disgust, and released her with so much force that Julie fell back against the bed. She was trembling so much that she had to sit down. This was awful—dreadful— worse than anything she had ever imagined having to face. She had known that Judy was sexually promiscuous, of course, but not this. Poor James. He had loved her so very much. Thank goodness he had never known what she was really like. It also answered the riddle of why Rocco had never questioned the discrepancy in their names. Judy had used Julie's name while in Cannes, betraying her yet again. Hot tears seared the backs of Julie's eyes.

'Did you tell James how you spent your time in Cannes?' Rocco demanded, as though he had somehow guessed the direction of her own thoughts.

'That's none of your business,' Julie told him, almost spitting the words at him in her determination to protect the man she had loved.

'That's where you're wrong. You've made it my business by being here. Did you plan the whole thing between you? You and this James? Did he procure you for Antonio, setting him up so that the pair of you could blackmail him with the threat of a child? That would certainly make you two of a kind.'

Julie sprang up off the bed, her face burning with the heat of her anger.

'James was a decent, kind and gentle man. He was worth a thousand men like you and your half-brother—arrogant, selfish, emotionally barren men, who think they can buy whatever they want.'

'What? You *dare* to put me in the same category as Antonio?'

'Why not?' Julie shot back. 'You both carry the same blood in your veins, after all.'

'Why, you—'

He was bending over her, dragging her to her feet. Frantically Julie fought to break free of his manacling grip on her wrists.

'I loved James,' she told him. 'But someone like you could never understand that.' Her voice caught and then broke.

Stifling an oath, Rocco released one of her wrists to cup her chin and lift it, so that he could look into her eyes. She looked like a martyr, all trampled pride and virtue, defending a lost love.

'You say that now,' he told her savagely, 'but you were still prepared to give yourself to me.'

'No. I loathe the thought of you touching me.'

'Like this, you mean?'

He was going to regret this when he had calmed down, Rocco knew, but right now his pride was asserting its need to be assuaged in a way that was driving out everything else.

Whilst she protested, he bent his head and silenced her with the pressure of his mouth on hers.

Julie told herself that she didn't want him, that she truly did loathe him, but some irresistible form of alchemy was taking place, transforming those feelings into their exact opposite. Her free hand lifted to his jaw—rough with nearly a full day's growth of beard, prickling the tender pads of her fingertips—to keep his mouth on her own.

Her heart was jerking in hot, tight spasms that echoed the speed with which the dull, heavy weight of the ache in her lower body was growing.

Rocco had released her other wrist to tangle his hand in her hair. He spread it flat against the back of her head, holding her beneath his kiss whilst his tongue prised open her lips.

Her heart shuddered, and burst into a flurry of heavy beats. The dull ache low down in her body spread to her thighs. Her tongue found his and she explored it with delicate little touches of her own tongue. She and James had never kissed like this. She had wanted to, but James had never initiated the intimacy.

Her heart slalomed as Rocco curled his tongue round her own, stroking it rhythmically, making her whole body move against his in an answering rhythm.

When had he last found this kind of sensuality in a kiss? Rocco wondered, already knowing the answer to his own question. Her response to him was sending rivers of molten desire speeding through him, destroying every obstacle in their way. Wasn't it more a matter of admitting that he had *never* found it—had never known that it could be found or that he wanted to find it—until now?

Rocco cupped the side of Julie's face with his free hand and kissed the tender spot just behind her ear, stroking it with his tongue tip.

Violent shudders of pleasure rocked through

Julie's body. She turned her face into Rocco's hand, caressing his fingers with her tongue, feeling the need inside her building to a hot, tight pulse.

Frantically she pushed Rocco away, catching him off guard.

'What is it?' His voice was raw and thick with arousal, and his hands returned to her body, shaping her waist, moving upward towards her breasts.

'I can't bear it,' Julie told him desperately, too caught up in the intensity of what she was feeling to hold back the truth. 'I don't want to feel like this. I don't want to want you so much. It's too much.' She trembled visibly.

The heaviness of her longing lay within her like an alien life form, possessing and controlling her. She looked at his hand, wondering what he would do if she reached for it and placed it against her sex, where the pulse of her desire had gone from a small flutter to a fierce, almost painful clamour. She felt lost, afraid, and terribly alone, in a place that was totally alien to all her previous experience, taken there by her desire for a man she didn't want to want.

How the hell did she expect him to back off after

saying something like that to him? Never mind when she was looking at him in the way that she was—as though all she wanted was to be possessed by him? Rocco wondered grimly. He felt his self-control give way beneath the combined weight of her words and his own desire.

'*You* are too much,' he told her thickly. 'Too much for me to resist.'

His hold encircled her, his hands sweeping up over her ribcage beneath the silky-fine knit of her top, pushing aside the decorative rather than practical barrier of her bra. His heat invaded her skin, branding his touch upon it. Her breasts, turgid now with desire, welcomed the cupped pressure of his hands, whilst the kisses he skimmed along the length of her neck and into her shoulder set off a reaction that burned its way through every sensory nerve ending her body possessed, so that her whole body vibrated visibly in mute shudders to the music of his touch, like an instrument played by a master musician.

Here on this island, with its buried veins of molten lava that ran so deep and possessed such danger, she was, Julie recognised distantly, finally discovering the hidden depths of her own passion. Like someone standing on its edge, looking down into the sleeping heart of the volcano, oblivious to its true nature, she had stood for so long on the edge of her own passions that she had overlooked how powerful they were.

Now, like lava running hot from deep down inside the earth, this man—a man whose blood and history had made him part of this island of volcanic uncertainty—was deliberately inciting her own fevered desire to the point where she could no longer control it. She could feel the need building up inside her—overpowering, commanding, demanding that she give herself over to it and to the man who had aroused it.

What was it about this woman that enabled her to transform herself into this living, breathing embodiment of such erotic and intense sensual responsiveness? He asked himself. It was as though she knew his every need, and could answer it in a way that took him deeper than he had ever previously gone into the molten heart of his own desire.

What her touch, her flesh, her self were drawing from him could never have been conjured up by mere sexual experience or tired, over-used mechanical responses of the 'you touch me like this and I respond like this' variety.

Somehow she was able to imbue even something as simple as the unsteady breath of her heartbeat against his flesh with such passion that her pleasure seemed new and tumultuous—an acknowledgement of a gift from him that took her into sensual realms she had never known before. Just the heavy-lidded and helplessly liquid look of longing that seemed to be dragged from her as though her need for him completely overwhelmed her was a form of arousal, and it took him in turn to a pitch that promised—and threatened—a degree of pleasure that challenged his own self-control.

When his touch had brought her to a state of semi-collapse, to lie boneless and mutely imploring against him, Rocco removed her top and then her bra, before sliding off her linen trousers.

Below the twin concave dips on either side of the minute swell of her stomach, he could see quite clearly, through the sheer fabric of her knickers and the more intimate covering of silky blonde hair that covered her sex, the frantic fast pulse of her need.

Rocco closed his eyes protectively and took a deep breath that lifted his torso, exhaling slowly as he fought for the command of himself that he could feel slipping away. But it was no good. The minute his eyelids lifted his gaze and returned it to that pulse, his whole body reacted to it.

He started to undress, unfastening just a few buttons on his shirt before he stopped, driven by his own need to lean forward and place his palms flat on the bed on either side of her hips, so that he could lower his head and feel that pulse, with its message of sensual untrammelled heat, against his mouth, so that he could take it deep inside himself to where his own body ached in exactly the same way.

Julie heard herself cry out—a sharp, keening sound somewhere between uncontrollable longing and helpless recognition that she was lost now to any kind of self-restraint.

The heat of Rocco's mouth penetrated the fine fabric covering her sex, making her feel as though she was melting inside, turning wet and soft, her flesh yearning.

When Rocco straightened up she wanted to protest, to beg him to continue. A wild, feverish and driving clamour of physical urgency was possessing her, causing her to move restlessly on the bed. The small out-of-control movements of her body reflected her impatience and her need, but then she realised that Rocco was removing his clothes, and her movements stilled. Her concentration was focused on watching as he shrugged off his shirt. The late afternoon sunlight breaking through the clouds strobed golden bars of light against his naked torso— honey against amber, sleeked with silk and velvet darkness where his body hair arrowed down beneath the waistband of the trousers he was now unfastening.

At some point he had removed his shoes, and for some reason the sight of his feet, bare, tanned and masculine, caused her heart to flip over. It was laughable, really, that such a small intimacy should possess such an intense charge. Was it because when James had made love to her he had never properly undressed, claiming that his shared student digs made it unwise? Did the sight of Rocco's bare feet somehow signal to her senses that now at last they would be able to experience what true sexual passion and the possession that went with it really meant?

Was it true after all that one did not need to be in love to enjoy passionate sex? Did she care?

Rocco stepped out of his trousers. Julie's heart took a high dive into shuddering delight. She had seen adverts for men's underwear, featuring what she had always suspected must surely be digitally honed and enhanced male models, but now she realised they had come nowhere even close to reflecting anything like the degree of male sexual perfection that was Rocco Leopardi. And how well that name suited him. Like the leopard, his flesh clung to sensuously strong muscles that moved sinuously and gracefully: a hunter's body, dangerously sleek with strength and purpose, its flesh satin-smooth, making her ache to reach out and stroke her hand against it.

When he removed his sleek-fitting white boxer shorts Julie sucked in her breath.

Had she actually ever seen James naked? If so, suddenly she not only couldn't remember but didn't really care. This—Rocco's body—was surely physically male sexual perfection? She had never given any thought to wondering if one day she might look at a naked man and want to feast her gaze on his sexuality. She simply hadn't thought in those kind of terms. She had loved James as a person, not for sex, and she was not the kind of woman who had ever been interested in going on a girls' night out to watch male strippers. She had believed that desiring a man came from loving him, but now, shockingly, she realised that just looking at Rocco was making her feel positively faint with lust.

Rocco watched Julie looking at him with a slanting half-hidden glance. Her lips were parted, her tongue pushing between them to dampen them, and her heart was thudding visibly and unevenly against her ribs. Her nipples were gathered and hard, but it was the look of open and awed delight he could see in her eyes that his own flesh registered first and responded to.

It was a look that said she was paying him the greatest compliment a woman could pay a man who had not yet been her lover. A look that aroused him even as it honoured and welcomed him.

He lay down on the bed beside her, kissing her slowly and with deliberately erotic intensity, using his tongue to tease and enflame her until she was reaching for him, her hands curling into the hard muscles of his arms, her mouth opening beneath his and her body arching up against him in open abandonment.

He cupped her breast and rubbed the pad of his thumb against her nipple as he kissed her neck, and then her shoulder, feeling her whole body jerk up against him in hot pleasure. He took her hand, lacing his fingers with her own and kissing the inside of her wrist as he played sensually with her nipple, before drawing her hand down to place it against his erection.

She made a semi-mute sound, her eyes widening as though with confusion and uncertainty. Her fingers trembled as they brushed against him, and then closed round him whilst she released her breath in a ragged exhalation.

His flesh felt hot and slick and heavy, moving almost of its own volition within her hold, causing her hand to tighten around it in possessive female delight. She released him to touch and stroke the full length of him, from the hard and shiny tip to the thick hair growing round the base that prickled against her fingers and then back again, until the sensation of his mouth against her breasts pierced her with such unbearable pleasure that her hand automatically gripped him. She was unable to enclose him fully, but still she tightened her fingers around him as the movement of her hand mirrored the slow, deep tug of his mouth against her nipple.

Rocco reached down and slid his hand into the open silk organza leg of her knickers, probing the already swollen and unfolding protective outer lips of her sex. Just as her tongue-tip had tempted him earlier, so the hard arousal of her clitoris tempted him now.

What was Rocco doing? James had never... But of course she knew what he was doing, Julie realized, and as she lay back, panting softly under the intensity her own pleasure. She wasn't that naïve, even if she had not experienced such a pleasure before. It gripped her and took her, softening some muscles and tightening others, opening her legs, lifting her hips, making her tremble violently, ready to throw herself into the heart of the volcano if necessary, rather than be denied pleasure.

Pleasure that Rocco's touch was promising her with a long, lazy caress that went the full length of her eager wetness in a way that made her ache and long feverishly for the thrust of his flesh within her own. She opened to his touch and cried out beneath the onslaught of sensation, her senses overloaded by the movement of his fingers against her clitoris.

Impatiently Rocco tugged off Julie's silky knickers, and then tensed as he realised what he was doing. She was lying naked and ready for him, her hips arched to allow him to remove her underwear, exposed intimately to his gaze. He tracked the frantic and unsteady pulse he could see beating beneath her skin. He didn't have a condom, and he didn't trust her. She had been his half-brother's plaything, and that of heaven alone knew how many other men. It was unthinkable that he could want her—and even if he did it was more unthinkable that he should take the risk involved in having sex with her. He started to move away from her, and then checked when she made a small agonised sound.

She was looking at him with helpless need and longing, pleading silently with him, pain and pride mingling with her shock at the extent of her wanting. She wasn't making any attempt to hide from him what was happening to her. The look on her face could have been that of a virgin who had never known such pleasures before, who was still half-afraid of them. But of course she was no such thing.

Rocco sighed and placed his hand on her thigh to push it closed against its twin, so that he could reject her without having to say the words he knew would humiliate her. Where had it come from, this extraordinary feeling he had of wanting to be gentle, of not wanting to hurt her? And more importantly why?

Her eyes closed, tears seeping from their corners, and a deep shudder racked through her.

She was in his hands—literally as well as figuratively. His to take or leave; his to pleasure or leave unfulfilled; his…

Something about her need for him, and the manner in which she was so helplessly vulnerable to it and to him reached out to him, touching his heart and making it impossible for him to deny her.

Rocco leaned over her, kissing her closed eyelids, tasting the salt of her tears, stroking her until her flesh quickened to his touch beyond the point of no recall.

It should have ended there, with the sound of her ragged breathing soft in his ear and the frantic pump of her heart easing back under the post-orgasm tremors seizing her body. He had, after all, given her what she had wanted, but in doing so he had unleashed his own passion, and now it was his turn to ache and burn for her beyond sanity or safety.

Her arms held him, wrapping around him. Her body was sweat-slick against his own. He lifted her hips and gave in to his need to sink into her, slowly, deeply, letting the mind-destroying pleasure take him as her flesh caressed him, her muscles holding him tighter than he had imagined possible.

How was it possible for a woman of her experience to show so little artifice? To be so held in the grip of her desire that her awe of it shone in her eyes and echoed in her soft cries of pleasure? How was it possible for her to be so sweetly shocked by the way he filled her, murmuring incoherent words of admiration and delight into his ear whilst her lips pressed eager kisses against his flesh? How was it possible—?

But anything and everything was possible

when a woman aroused a man the way she had aroused him, Rocco acknowledged as he let the fire take him and burn him, commanding his thrusts and his rhythm in the same way that he was commanding her response to them, possessing thcm both and driving them through urgency and need to the heart of their shared desire. The volcanic explosion that brought his climax a second ahead of hers let him feel the pressure of her flesh gripping him and releasing him in swift convulsive movements.

It was over, leaving her boneless, mindless… and heartless? Julie closed her eyes. Her body was too sated by the extraordinarily intense power of her orgasm for her to have the energy to think. She reached out and let her fingers drift down Rocco's back, damp with the sweat she could still taste on her own lips. She felt humbled and awed, almost unable to believe she had known so much pleasure, and she was hugely grateful to fate for giving her both the opportunity to do so and the man who could arouse it as she lay in a post-coital state of euphoric bliss.

Rocco had given her something that James

never had, and she would always be grateful to him, and to life, for that.

The post-orgasm scent of their bodies surrounded her, soothing and relaxing. Julie closed her eyes and moved closer to Rocco, burrowing against him, wanting to be close to him…

She was nothing like he had imagined, he thought. She was a voluptuous innocent who had somehow undermined his defences and taken him to a place he had never previously been.

A voluptuous innocent? She was practically a whore, Rocco reminded himself grimly, and if she seemed innocent it was probably because she was experienced enough to know that men who should know better were turned into helpless fools by her toxic masquerade.

And yet still he couldn't bring himself to leave her…

CHAPTER NINE

JULIE'S hands trembled as she fastened Josh's nappy and paused to blow a kiss at him as he looked back at her and smiled. Today was the day they would learn the results of the DNA tests, and in fact the doctor was due in less than half an hour, according to the message Maria had given her from Rocco at breakfast time.

Rocco. Julie hadn't been alone with him since she had gone to sleep in his arms two days ago. It was quite clear what message he wanted to send to her. She had known that the moment she had woken up in the dark alone.

Perhaps she should feel ashamed of what she had done? Rocco probably thought so, but Julie wasn't ashamed. She wasn't ashamed of anything—not a single, wonderful second of it. She had wanted to know the depth and breadth of her own sensuality and now she did. And if

Rocco Leopardi thought that that meant she was going to pursue him for more of the same then he couldn't be more wrong.

One day maybe she would meet someone with whom she could fall in love in the same way that she had fallen in love with James, but this time she would know her own sexual nature, and its needs.

Poor James. He had hated hurting people so very much, and she suspected now that he had probably allowed her to believe that he loved her rather than hurt her with the truth that he merely liked her as a person rather than desired her as a woman. His love for her, she was sure, had been that of a friend, not a lover. That made her feel sad and regretful—more for her lack of understanding and awareness than anything else. But the anger she had felt was gone—swept away in the torrent of passion she had known beneath Rocco's hands and in his arms.

She picked Josh up and cuddled him, in part to distract herself from the direction of her thoughts and to conceal her faint blush, although she never needed an excuse to show her love for her precious nephew. He was growing bigger by the day now, putting on weight and responding to the attention she gave him with smiles and joy that turned her heart over, until it felt as though it was melting with her love for him.

There was nothing she wouldn't do for him to keep him safe and well.

She wished the ordeal ahead of her was already over, and that she knew one way or the other where Josh's future lay: here in Sicily or at home in London. But wherever it was she intended to be with him.

'You're my baby,' she whispered lovingly to him. 'My adorable, gorgeous, wonderful baby.'

His chuckle made her laugh and Rocco, who had heard both her words and her soft loving laughter, paused on the landing outside her bedroom on his way past, immediately rejecting the sensation that tightened round his heart.

She meant nothing to him. How could she? He just hoped that her child would *not* turn out to be Antonio's son. That way he could have her on the first flight back to London so that he could get on with his life and forget that he had ever met her, his duty to his family done.

And if the boy *was* Antonio's?

The same thing applied. He had his own life.

She and the boy would become his father's responsibility, not his, and the castle her home—if his father allowed her to stay.

It was almost eleven o'clock. He'd been out at the development since seven o'clock, and he needed a shower before Luca arrived. Rocco rubbed his hand over his jaw. He hadn't been sleeping well, waking up in the night with an ache in his body and a sense of loss and aloneness.

He cursed himself under his breath. Wasn't it bad enough that he'd had unprotected sex with a party girl, without developing some maudlin sense of thinking that his bed felt empty without her in it?

Julie tried to smile naturally as she walked into the salon which she had previously considered to be the most 'homely' of all the villa's formal reception rooms, but which now felt formidably grand.

Dr Vittorio and Rocco were already there. The doctor was formally dressed in a dark suit, in contrast to Rocco, who was wearing a soft, white, short-sleeved cotton top and a pair of clean but slightly faded chinos. His hair looked damp, as though he had recently been in the shower. Her belly cramped, her muscles compressing against the now-familiar ache that accompanied his presence in her thoughts.

Whilst the doctor smiled at her Rocco came forward, taking Josh out of her arms before she could protest.

Apprehension surged through her, leaching the blood from under her skin and leaving it milk-white.

Had the doctor already given Rocco the results of the tests? Had he taken Josh from her because—?

Maria's entrance with coffee and some of her homemade almond biscuits, plus—thoughtfully—a bottle for Josh, cranked up Julie's tension.

Maria had poured their coffee and left them before Dr Vittorio reached for his leather case and opened it, saying calmly, 'Since I know you will both be anxious to hear the results of the tests, I will not delay any longer.'

He looked at Julie, giving her a look that made her heart turn over. It contained compassion and, she thought, regret. She watched him remove some papers from his case and hand them each a set.

'You will both see for yourselves that the tests show quite clearly that Antonio is not Josh's father.'

Not his father! Julie's hand trembled, her whole body going weak with relief. The papers she was holding slipped from her grasp. She had to sit down. Only now could she admit how much she had wanted this result—and not just because she'd wanted to believe that James was Josh's father. It was for Josh's own sake that she did not want him to have been fathered by Antonio Leopardi.

And for her own? Because she didn't think she could trust herself if she had to remain in close proximity to Rocco Leopardi?

Rocco frowned as he saw Julie's reaction, his frown deepening when Luca helped her to one of the hard-backed satin-covered sofas, urging her to sit down.

Still holding Josh, Rocco went towards them, bending down to pick up the papers she had dropped as he did so. He registered both how much thicker the set she had was, compared with his own, and then the look of concern on Luca's face as he stepped forward to say, 'Let me take that for you, Rocco.' He reached not for Josh, but for the DNA document.

Julie leaned back against the sofa. It was over.

Josh was hers and only hers. The relief was making her feel slightly sick, as though it was almost too rich for her to digest.

Ignoring Luca's words, Rocco flipped over the printed sheets of data. The first one was an exact copy of his own, but the second was different.

He had to read what it said twice before he could rationalise it, then his mouth thinned as he looked first at Luca and then across to where Julie was leaning back against the sofa with her eyes closed.

Luca placed a restraining hand on Rocco's arm, his expression one of concern and disquiet, but Rocco ignored his silent message, shaking off his hand and striding over to the sofa.

She had nothing to fear from Rocco now, Julie reassured herself, reaching up to take Josh from him, assuming that that was the only reason he had come over to her despite the look of compressed anger he was giving her. But instead of handing Josh to her he sat down beside her, still holding him in the crook of his arm whilst with the other hand he waved the papers he was gripping in front of her.

'What the hell does this mean?' he demanded.

Julie looked at him blankly, and Dr Vittorio interceded warningly. 'Rocco, Julie hasn't seen the results herself yet.'

'She doesn't need to see them, does she? After all, she knows perfectly well already that she isn't Josh's mother.'

Julie gasped and looked helplessly at the doctor, who shrugged in apology and told her, 'I'm sorry—I should have warned you. But I didn't give Rocco a set of your results. Since I was going to talk to you later about your own health, I had planned to mention it to you then.'

'So if you aren't Josh's mother then who the hell are you?' Rocco demanded, barely waiting for the doctor to finish speaking before he fired his furious question at her.

Rocco still had Josh cradled in the crook of his arm. Julie wanted very badly to take her nephew from him, but to do so she would have to reach across Rocco himself.

It was easier to say huskily instead, 'Please give Josh to me.'

'Why? He isn't your child.'

It was as though he wanted to hurt her—his words a deliberate blow, a rejection of her place in Josh's life. But why? Josh meant nothing to him. He wasn't Antonio's child after all. The DNA tests had proved that as conclusively as they had obviously also proved that she wasn't his mother.

'Not my child, no,' Julie agreed, her chin firming with determination as she confronted him. 'But he is related to me—I am his aunt.'

'His aunt?'

'Yes.'

'So where's his real mother? Or can I guess? Living it up with the man she found to take Antonio's place—if indeed it is only one man. What do the pair of you do? Take it in turns to live the good life?'

Julie had had enough—more than enough, in fact.

'You have no right to say that. You don't know anything about me or the way I live my life.'

Colour stained her skin as she saw the manner in which he was looking at her. She knew he wanted to remind her of what had happened between them, and how she had abandoned herself to his lovemaking. It had been a lie to say that he knew nothing about her. Of course he knew something about her—he knew a great deal about her in one sense. Certainly more than any other man did. Maybe more than any other man ever would. There wouldn't be many men prepared to take on a young woman with a child—especially when they learned the story of Josh's conception and she was obliged to admit that she had no idea who had fathered him. It was too late now to wish, as she had so passionately on many occasions these last few days, that she had thought to ask for DNA tests to be done herself to see if James was Josh's father. Unfortunately at the time of his death the issue of Josh's paternity had been the last thing on her mind.

Julie exhaled shakily. 'My sister is not partying.' Her voice twisted. 'And before you ask me how I can be so sure about that, the reason I know is that she is dead.'

Julie bent her head, concentrating on watching the way her fingers pleated the silky fabric of her long cardigan as carefully as though her life depended upon it.

'Judy—my sister—our parents, James—her fiancé—and his parents were all killed in a rail accident earlier this year. They were going to Scotland to look at a castle Judy had read about as a possible venue for their wedding. They'd left Josh with me because—'

'Because your sister didn't want to be bothered with him.'

The ugly brutality of Rocco's statement fell painfully across her heart.

'It is difficult, when you've got something as important as a wedding to plan, to look after a small baby, and Josh hadn't been very well. Our parents agreed that for his own sake he should be left with me.'

'So it was your sister who was Josh's mother, and presumably Antonio's bed-mate?'

'Yes. She told me about him. And…and about the fact that she was pregnant.'

'Did she tell you he was the father?'

'She thought he might be,' Julie replied carefully. Thanks to Rocco, she now knew just what her sister had been doing whilst she had been in Cannes, and so could understand why Judy hadn't been sure who'd fathered Josh, telling her that she only *thought* that Antonio could be the father of the child she was carrying.

'You mentioned a fiancé?'

'James? Yes.'

'James.'

The way Rocco said James's name told Julie that he had recognised it—and why.

'Tell me something. When you referred to James in our discussions were you referring to him in your assumed role as your sister or on your own behalf?'

Julie frowned.

'I'm sorry—I don't quite understand.'

'Was he your lover or your sister's?' he demanded bluntly.

Julie could feel the raw burn of her own humiliation.

Lifting her head, she faced him squarely and told him quietly, 'He was my lover first and then Judy's. Not that it is really any of your business.'

She wasn't going to explain or attempt to defend herself. Let him believe what he wanted to believe.

Dr Vittorio, who had moved over to the window, must have moved back, because Julie heard him saying firmly, 'Rocco, that's enough, I think. All you really have a right or a need to know is that Julie here is the little one's blood relative.'

'And his legal guardian,' Julie put in determinedly.

'I need to speak with Julie about her own
health, but first I'm afraid there's something else
I should tell you. Your father rang me this
morning, insisting that I tell him the results of the
DNA tests.'

'And did you?'

'Yes—since he was working himself up into a bit
of a state, and it had in fact been proved that Josh
is not his grandson. He is naturally disappointed.'

He certainly would be, Rocco reflected, but if
he was honest he felt relieved for little Josh's
sake. At least now the child would be spared
over-indulgence coupled with emotional ma-
nipulation—which, Rocco and his brothers
believed, had led to Antonio turning into the
adult he had become.

Julie was grateful to the doctor for having taken
Rocco's attention from her, and even more
grateful when he asked quietly if he could talk to
her in private about the results of her blood tests.

She was just about to nod her head when
Rocco shocked her, by confronting the doctor
and telling him crisply, 'Patient confidentiality

is all very well, Luca, but since I have a vested interest in Julie's health, I should warn you that I intend to be made fully aware of her results *and* your diagnosis.'

In saying that he had a 'vested interest' in her health, was he reminding her that he had paid Dr Vittorio's fees? Julie wondered uncomfortably. It was humiliating to know that she simply could not afford to stand up and tell him that she would pay her own bills and buy Josh's and her own clothes.

'Julie must give her permission.'

They were both looking at her.

He knew the secret she had been keeping from him now, so what was the point in refusing? Except, of course, for the boost it would give her pride. Until he pointed out that she had no money to pay the doctor's bill.

'I don't know why you should be interested in my health,' she told Rocco, before turning away to look up at the doctor and say quietly, 'But, since obviously you are, then, yes, Dr Vittorio— I give my permission.'

The doctor opened his bag again and withdrew a file of papers, giving Julie a brief, reassuring smile as he saw the anxious look she gave it.

'You are, as I thought, suffering from anaemia,' he told her. 'But as the blood tests I ordered have not shown cause for concern in the form of any kind of serious medical complaint which could have led to problems with your blood cell count, I think we must put your condition down to other influences. You are a young woman in sole charge of a small child, with no partner or family to support you. You told me yourself that Josh had health problems of his own, and I can guess that the deaths of so many people close to you must have had a traumatic effect. If in addition to that you have perhaps had financial problems...' He paused tactfully, whilst the colour came and went in Julie's face.

'I... The nature of the deaths of my sister and our parents has meant that there will be delays in sorting things out. Josh and I are, of course, the sole beneficiaries of my parents' estate, but my parents' will did not cover this kind of eventuality. My solicitor is doing his best, but he doesn't know how long it will be before we are able to receive anything. I did have some savings—not much, and when Josh was ill I had to take time off work. Then...' She bit her lip, not wanting to betray Judy. 'There were certain monies owing that had to be paid.'

'You mean that your sister left you her debts?' Rocco challenged her.

'Not deliberately. Judy didn't know what was going to happen.'

'She knew she had a child to support, and that she was shortly to get married.'

'Things *have* been difficult,' Julie admitted to the doctor, ignoring Rocco.

'There is no real serious problem with your health, but I do not wish to minimise the danger of your anaemia. You really do need to eat properly and rest. Some warm sunshine and freedom from the burden of the worries you have been carrying would do a great deal to improve things.'

Julie managed a small smile.

'I shall do my best to follow your advice,' she told him, turning back to Rocco to say coolly, 'Now that Josh has been ruled out as a potential Leopardi, I'd like to return to London as soon as possible. There's no need for us to remain here now.'

It was Rocco's turn not to answer. She was right. There was no reason for her to remain here now. His duty to his brothers and the Leopardi name was done; it only remained for him to inform Falcon of the results of the DNA tests.

There was, of course, the matter of their financially recompensing Julie for the disruption to her life—as Falcon had said they must if her child should prove not to be Antonio's.

Rocco started to frown. That should surely be his responsibility, since he was in the best position to judge what adequate recompense might be. Swiftly he mentally surveyed his memories of the area in which Julie and Josh lived, and their circumstances when he had found them, adding them to the information about her health that the doctor had just given them. He came to an immediate decision.

'On the contrary,' he corrected Julie tersely. 'There are two very good reasons why you should remain here, and I am surprised that you have not thought of them for yourself.'

Julie looked at him uncertainly and waited.

'I am sure that Dr Vittorio will agree with me that, given your own poor health—'

'My health is not poor. I am anaemic, that is all.'

Ignoring her outburst, Rocco continued, 'And given the fact that Josh is making such good progress here, it not only makes sense but in many ways I consider it essential that you should stay here until your health has improved.'

'I can't do that,' Julie protested. But even though she was saying the words, she knew perfectly well that there was nothing she really wanted more than to stay.

'Rocco is right.' Dr Vittorio joined the conversation, nodding his head. 'In fact, I cannot think of a better prescription for both you *and* Josh.'

'I have a job, and a flat, and…'

'You have a serious health problem which will surely deteriorate if you return too quickly to the life you were living. No, my mind is made up,' Rocco said firmly. 'You and Josh will remain here in Sicily until Dr Vittorio pronounces you well enough to leave.'

Julie gasped. Well, honestly—of all the arrogant, high-handed things to do! But what could she say? She knew Rocco well enough now to know that there was no point in arguing with him. And he was right about her health and about Josh. She would never forgive herself if she insisted on returning to London only to find that Josh's health started to deteriorate. How could she provide the kind of environment for him that he had here? And besides, if she stayed, then perhaps...

Perhaps what? Perhaps because Rocco had had sex with her it meant something? She would be foolish in the extreme to start believing that, Julie warned herself. He didn't care about her at all. And what was more she didn't care about him either. What they had shared had just been sex, and she had better not forget that.

Just? How could the word 'just' be applied to the wondrous life-changing experience she had had in his arms? But she must not admit to that. Not even to herself. In fact, she must not think about it at all.

It had been a tumultuously difficult morning, and Julie was relieved to finally be on her own with Josh, enjoying the sunshine in a sheltered part of the courtyard garden.

At least she *had* been enjoying it on her own. She grimaced, her heart sinking as she looked up and saw Rocco striding purposefully towards them. His shadow cast a long silhouette in front of him that touched her before he himself reached her, reminding her, if she had been in need of any reminder, that there was no part of her he himself had not touched—physically and emotionally.

'This James,' he demanded abruptly. 'You were in love with him?'

Julie looked away from him. Now what did he want?

'Yes,' she acknowledged.

'He was your first lover?'

Immediately she turned to look at him, the startled shock in her expression betraying her ahead of her reluctant, 'Yes.'

Josh, lying on his rug on top of a comfortably padded throw Maria had found for them, crowed in triumph as he found his own toes, momentarily distracting them both.

'Before you say anything, I've put sunscreen on him.' Julie rushed into the silence to defend herself from the question she suspected might be coming—only to stop, torn between discomfort and an unwanted feeling of sharp grief as she realised that there was no reason for Rocco to care what happened to her nephew anymore.

Perhaps, though, he was as slow to recognise

that fact as she had been, because he answered coolly, 'Maria said that you had. It's just as well that you are keeping him out of the direct sunlight, though. His skin won't be used to it.'

He turned back to her, resting one foot on a stone tortoise close to where she was sitting so that he could lean closer to her and demand, 'And he has been your only lover?'

Her heart jumped so much that it felt as though it had lodged in her throat.

'I can't see what relevance that could have to anything we might need to discuss.'

She'd been proud of the calm levelness of her voice, convinced that it hadn't given anything away, until he stood upright and said, in a voice that seemed oddly to hold satisfaction, 'So he has. And what happened? Obviously it wasn't anything to do with your lack of willingness in bed.'

Julie was torn between chagrin and indignation.

'What James and I felt for one other didn't have anything to do with sex,' she told him, only realising when it was too late, and one dark eyebrow had risen in a mocking gesture of cynicism, just how her defence could be interpreted. 'What I meant was that we loved one another and…and our relationship wasn't based merely on sex,' she corrected herself.

'You loved him but he didn't turn you on?'

'No! I mean, yes—I loved him and of course he turned me on.'

'So what happened?'

When she looked uncertainly at him he sat down on the stone bench next to her chair. 'What do you mean what happened?' she asked.

'You said that he was potentially Josh's father, and that he had been your sister's lover—which begs the question why? According to what you've just said, you loved one another and were already lovers.'

Julie looked at Josh. Watching him gave her a valid reason for not looking at Rocco.

'My sister was extremely beautiful. She liked to boast that she could have any man she wanted, and she wanted James.'

'Your sister was a tart, who traded sex for material possessions and a taste of the kind of life she lusted after more than she did the men foolish enough to find her attractive.'

'James fell in love with her,' Julie continued, refusing to argue with him. 'I was dreadfully hurt at the time. Poor James—it must have been so difficult for him. He knew how much I loved him, and he didn't want to hurt me, so…'

'So he continued to have sex with you as well as with her?'

'No!' Julie was too shocked to lie. 'No, of course not. There was no question of anything like that.'

Enlightenment dawned, and she gave him a bitter smile.

'If it's your health you're worrying about, and the reason for all these questions, I can assure you are quite safe from any contamination from me. I had a full check-up when I fell ill with a virus that I caught from Josh. My local surgery is involved in a government-sponsored drive to do that kind of thing.'

'You must have found it difficult to go without sex once he'd left you for your sister,' said Rocco, ignoring her bitter outburst.

His blunt comment made her feel defensive. 'Why do you say that?'

'Because you were so hungry for it with me,' he told her, even more bluntly. 'More hungry than I've ever known any other woman to be.'

'I'm sorry if you found my...me offensive.' Her voice was stiff with pride now.

'I didn't say that,' Rocco told her laconically. 'I simply said that you were desperately hungry for a man's touch and the satisfaction that goes with it.'

'I'd really rather we didn't discuss this subject anymore.' How prim she sounded. But what he was saying reminded her far too intimately of just how abandoned she had been.

Julie moved uncomfortably in her chair, the small movement watched thoughtfully by Rocco.

It had shocked him at first to discover that she wasn't the woman he had thought. But he couldn't deny that the discovery had made sense of several things about her that had puzzled him. Talking to her now had added a certain piquancy to what he already knew—like a delicate sauce added to a dish that was already tempting the appetite.

'Why didn't you tell me right from the start that you were not Josh's mother? It would certainly have saved us both a great deal of aggravation.'

'You didn't exactly give me the chance, did you? How could I, when you'd already made up your mind about me? Besides, I was afraid that if Josh did turn out to be your half-brother's child your family would take him away from me straight away if they knew I wasn't his mother.'

'I gave you my word that that would not happen,' Rocco pointed out.

'Well, I won't have to worry about it now, will I? Because Josh isn't Antonio's son, thank goodness. I always hoped that James would be his father.'

'Because you loved him?'

He was too astute.

'Yes,' she admitted. 'Not that I don't love Josh for his own sake. I do.'

She meant what she said, Rocco thought, watching her. Josh was very lucky to have a mother figure in his life who was so protective of him.

'There is still the matter of our recompensing you for coming here,' Rocco continued. 'I cannot say how much the sum will be until I have spoken with my eldest brother.'

'I don't want any money.' Julie could feel her heart thudding with angry pride.

'It has already been agreed that you will be recompensed. It is our duty to do so.'

How arrogant he sounded and looked. Julie's

throat ached with her own painful emotions. It was so easy for her to see how he viewed her. To him she was someone of no account, whose feelings did not matter—someone he could simply pay to disappear from his life.

'No. I will not take it.'

The ferocity and passion in her voice surprised Rocco.

'Why not? After all, you were quick enough to agree to come with me when I told you in London that there would be a financial advantage in your agreeing to come to Sicily with me.'

That was different, Julie wanted to tell him. That was before you touched me and I knew… But she must not admit even to herself what she knew.

'I thought you meant that Antonio had made some kind of financial provision for his child,' Julie said stiffly. It was in part the truth.

Rocco shrugged dismissively. 'So the money will come from us, Antonio's half-brothers, there is no difference.'

'Yes, there is,' Julie insisted. 'You talk of your own pride—the Leopardi pride—well, you are not the only person to have pride. I have it too, and I will not accept money. Josh is not a Leopardi.

My pride is every bit as important to me as yours is to you, and I do not want your money.'

To his shock Rocco realised that something— a combination of emotions that gripped his heart in some unfathomable way—was making him want to take hold of her and go on holding her. Determinedly, he pushed the feeling away.

'Maybe not, but you have Josh to think of.'

'It is because I am thinking of him. I don't want him growing up thinking that it is acceptable to live off other people. I want you to give me an account of everything you have spent on us so that I can repay you once my parents' estate is settled.'

'Absolutely not,' Rocco told her arrogantly. 'Your request is offensive, and an insult to me as a Leopardi.'

Julie's eyes widened. What about his offensiveness to her? she wanted to say, but she knew there was no point. Rocco might describe his father as arrogant but he himself was no better. Arrogant, high-handed, incredibly and overpoweringly sexy—

Julie clamped down on the unwanted thought that had somehow or other managed to slip past her defences.

Her defences? Why would she need to defend herself against acknowledging that Rocco was a very sexually attractive male?

Did she really need to ask herself that, when she didn't even have to see him or be with him to ache for a repeat of the pleasure he had already shown her?

CHAPTER TEN

IT HAD been Maria's idea, and her determined lobbying of Rocco on Julie and Josh's behalf, that had finally led to Rocco giving in and agreeing to take them both to watch the annual ceremonial parade in a small town ten miles away from the villa. Traditionally, to mark the start of spring and to bring luck for a good harvest to the town's surrounding citrus groves, the townspeople paraded through the town on floats and in costumes. The event was one of the highlights of the year in the area.

As though the weather was determined to be in accord with the date—and very auspiciously, according to Maria—they had woken up to brilliant sunshine and a warmth in the air which, combined with the scent of citrus, couldn't help but lift anyone's spirits, Julie admitted.

Julie had dressed Josh for the event in one of

his new outfits—a pair of neutral-coloured baby chinos, and a checked shirt in blue-greys and yellow, over which she had slipped a small matching pullover in blue-grey with a knitted yellow border. He looked absolutely adorable, Julie decided, and as though he knew that himself—or had picked up on her own excitement at the thought of having a day out—he was all beaming smiles.

But was her happy mood occasioned by the thought of a day out because she would be spending the day in Rocco's company? Julie asked herself sternly as she finished getting ready.

What if she *did* want to spend the day with Rocco? There was nothing wrong in that, was there? Julie's eyes widened slightly at her own naïveté. Of course there was something wrong with it. And what was wrong with it was the fact that she wanted to be with Rocco at all. She would soon be going home. Once she was back in London she would never see him again.

All the more reason to make any most of the opportunity to spend time with him now, the reckless voice inside her urged. Whilst that other voice, the one that knew her better, warned her that if she listened to its opponent she would end up being badly hurt.

It was foolish and dangerous to build fantasies inside her head that could never be anything *but* fantasy. So Rocco had made love to her and it had been a life-changing experience for her? That did not mean he felt the same way. For him it had simply been sex, and she must accept that and move on from it. Yes, now she knew what it was to be sexually fulfilled, and she could dream if she wished of how wonderful it would be one day to meet a man whom she could love sexually and emotionally, but she must accept that that man would not be Rocco.

By repeating that warning to herself when Rocco came to take Josh downstairs for her she was almost able to behave naturally, and as though the sensation of his hand brushing against her bare arm as he took the baby from her had absolutely no effect on her at all.

Although Maria had assured her that the parade had no religious significance, Julie had decided that it might be as well to cover up rather than risk causing any offence. She was wearing a pair of off-white linen trousers teamed with a cobalt-blue silky strappy top in case it got warm, with a matching prettily shaped knitted jacket over the top.

When she saw the way Rocco was looking at her she laughed and told him, 'Whoever selected these clothes obviously didn't realise they'd be worn by someone who spends her time with a small child. They are impractical, I know, but it's such a sunny day that I couldn't resist wearing them.'

'You've put on weight,' Rocco told her, ignoring her comment. 'Good. You needed to.'

'I suppose I *had* begun to look slightly scrawny,' she agreed.

'Not scrawny. That is an ugly word, and you could never look ugly.' Before she had time to register the fact that he was actually paying her a compliment he continued, 'Fragile is the word I would have used. Maria has told you, I expect, that she is joining her own family for the celebrations?'

Julie nodded her head.

'I should warn you that it will be very crowded; it is best, I think, that we stick together.'

The minute the local lotharios saw Julie on her

own they would home in on her like locusts, Rocco thought grimly. Had he ever actually thought of her as plain and dull? It wasn't just the little bit of much-needed weight she had put on that was responsible for the glow that now seemed to illuminate her face, Rocco suspected. The fact that she was now free from the pressure of having to struggle to support herself and Josh as well as pay off her late sister's debts must also have played its part.

They were in the car, Josh strapped into his baby seat and cooing happily to himself, and Julie couldn't help smiling herself.

How could he possibly not have recognised her beauty right from the start? Rocco asked himself. When she smiled, as she was doing now, she had such a serene look of joy about her that it caught at his heart and stopped his breath. Any man would be proud to call such a woman his own.

Now what was he thinking? Hadn't he always sworn that he would never marry or make a commitment to any woman?

It didn't take them long to reach their destination, and Julie gave a small exclamation of pleasure as she saw the ancient walls of the town rising from the rocks on which it was built, the grilled windows of the houses which had obviously been built into the walls over the years looking down at them.

'The present-day town was built on the site of an Arab fort,' Rocco explained, deciding that it would be wiser and safer for him to talk about the history of the town than to let his thoughts travel in the direction in which they seemed rebelliously determined to travel.

'As one of the conquering Normans who fought for and won the island, our ancestor was given land and this town—which he in turn fortified. It was only later that our family moved out of their fortified home here in the town to the castle—although of course we still retain strong links with the town. In fact, you will see signs of that everywhere—in the names of streets, in the Leopardi coat of arms on walls here and there, and some say in the faces of some of the townspeople as well, from the days when it was considered a matter of honour for the daughter of a family to be selected by her lord to warm his bed for a season.'

Julie winced. Small wonder, with a family history such as the one Rocco was so casually outlining, that he should think nothing of taking her to bed.

Rocco parked the car on a piece of flat ground which was obviously serving as a temporary car park. 'The streets of the town are very narrow, and whilst traffic is not prohibited it is not encouraged. In the summer as well as now, during the festival, it attracts a good many visitors—all the more so since Falcon persuaded our father to allow work to begin on the restoration of the ancient steam and mud baths. Legend has it that the Greek architect Daedalus designed the building which surrounds them after he fled here from Crete. The restoration work is due to be completed this year.'

'It sounds fascinating,' Julie told him truthfully, holding Josh whilst Rocco dealt with the buggy.

As they joined the stream of people walking towards the main gated entrance to the town, Julie reflected that they could have been any small family on a day out—except for the fact that it was plain to her from the looks Rocco was attracting that most people knew who he was and were slightly in awe of him. And of course she was nothing to him other than someone who might have been the mother of his half-brother's illegitimate child.

What was it, she wondered, about a certain kind of man that automatically set him apart and elevated him from other men, causing his own sex to view him with respect and her own with animated delight? Whatever it was, Rocco certainly had that quality in spades. The Leopardis might be lords of all they could survey here in this part of Sicily, but Rocco had no need of the Leopardi name to attract female interest or to prove that he was an alpha male, Julie thought ruefully. Even the way he pushed the buggy somehow reinforced and emphasised his maleness.

The place to watch the parade was in the *piazza* in front of the town's main church, according to Maria, and it was there that Julie and Rocco headed, to rendezvous with the housekeeper and her family.

Their progress was held up by the number of people who came forward to pay their respects to Rocco, but finally they reached the square, guided through the crowd by two young men who had introduced themselves as Maria's grandsons, with the information that Maria and her family had saved them a grandstand view.

A grandstand view would have been found for Rocco in any case, Julie guessed—which made it all the more touching to see the way in which he courteously thanked Maria for her trouble.

Josh had to be admired by Maria's female relatives and passed round amongst them in a way that slightly alarmed Julie at first—until she reminded herself that this would be the custom in a large family clan, and it would be churlish to make a fuss.

By the time the parade started Josh was back in her arms, wide awake and gazing around— although of course he was far too young to be aware of what was happening.

For sheer pageantry the parade took one's breath away, Julie admitted, wincing slightly at the noise from the trumpets of the brightly clothed heralds in their scarlet and gold tabards, followed by 'men at arms' dragging 'prisoners', and then floats filled with people in all manner of costumes.

On the other side of the square, during a small

gap in the parade, Julie watched as a young couple embraced, the girl turning her face for her partner's kiss. Their happiness, so very evident and joyous, made her feel very alone.

Someone wanting to get closer to the parade pushed past her, causing her to half stumble into Rocco. As he steadied her Julie started to apologise, but Rocco shook his head, telling her calmly as he put his arm round her waist and drew her closer to him, 'Whilst we're in this crowd I think it would be safer if you stood close to me.'

Since Rocco had already reached for the buggy with his free hand, whilst keeping his arm around her, Julie had no option but to stay where she was.

She would be safer, Rocco had said. Safe from being accidentally pushed by the crowd, perhaps, but certainly not safe from an even greater danger. The scent of his cologne, so barely and yet so tantalisingly discernible against all the stronger smells of hot food and sunshine, made her want to turn her head so that she could seek it out and breathe it in. But would she be able to stop at that? Wouldn't she then be tempted to nuzzle the warm column of his throat, exploring it with her kisses and all the time moving closer to his mouth? Her heart slammed into her ribs, desire curling insidiously through her body as light as smoke and as dangerous as fire.

'You are enjoying the parade?' Rocco asked, his lips close to her ear so that she could hear him above the noise of the crowd.

Of course it was to hear him that she half turned into his body. His hand was a warm heavy weight against her hip, and Julie was thankful that he didn't know that the ache in her breasts and the ache in her lower body were in competition over which was most intensely in need of the touch of his hand.

When it was time for them to go and have some lunch Julie didn't know whether to be relieved or disappointed that there was no longer any need for them to share such physical intimacy.

It had been a wonderful day—a special, magical day out of time—and she would treasure its memory for ever, Julie decided happily later on in the afternoon, as she and Rocco made their way back to the car. Rocco was pushing the buggy, and when he reached for her hand to help her over a patch of rocky ground, then kept on holding it, Julie felt her heart somersault with delight.

They were back at the villa when Julie's happiness was suddenly changed to shocked fear and disbelief.

The bleep of her mobile phone warning her of a voicemail message was unusual enough to have her immediately removing the phone from her handbag, and she excused herself to Rocco when she saw that the message was from her solicitor.

It was long and complex, and the news it contained was dreadful. It drove the happy pink flush of colour from her face, and she had to hear it again to make sure she had not misunderstood it.

Her solicitor reported that, due to the fact that her parents had remortgaged their house a year before their deaths and given a very large sum of money to Judy, and also the fact that for some reason her father had omitted to pay the premiums on his life insurance, there would be very little value in their estate for Julie and Josh to inherit.

And, if that was not bad enough, he added that he also had to inform Julie that a solicitor for James's sister and her husband had been in touch, advising that they intended to ask the courts to revoke Julie's status as Josh's legal guardian in their favour because they did not think that as a single young woman she could provide the same quality of care and financial security for Josh as they could.

The fact that they were a couple and were far more comfortably circumstanced than she was herself, thus better able to provide Josh with a stable and secure home, meant that in his view their challenge had to be taken very seriously indeed, her solicitor warned her, adding that the process would be a long and very expensive one, and that in the circumstances Julie might want to think seriously about where Josh's best long-term interests lay.

In other words, her solicitor thought that she should give Josh up.

'No!' The mobile slipped through her fingers to fall on the floor whilst Julie sat down on the stairs and covered her face with her hands.

Rocco scooped up the mobile, checking that Josh was still safely asleep in his buggy. When Julie failed to respond he autocratically listened to the message himself, and strode towards her.

Somehow she had managed to get herself under control and stand up, even though she felt sick with shock and despair. What was she going to do?

'I don't understand,' she told Rocco. 'Annette doesn't even like children. She's always refused to have a family, even though her husband desperately wants one. She wouldn't even look at Josh, never mind hold him. She told me to keep him away from her in case he dirtied her expensive coat. I can't let her take him. She won't love him properly. I know she won't.'

Her shocked distress aroused all Rocco's protective instincts. He had grown up without his own mother and he knew the pain that caused. Josh had already bonded with Julie, and the truth was that he had grown attached to the child himself. Why should Josh be handed over to strangers just because they were a couple, when he could provide him not only with financial security but also with a father?

'There is a solution,' he told Julie, his mind made up.

'What?'

'Marriage.'

CHAPTER ELEVEN

'MARRIAGE,' Julie repeated uncomprehendingly.

'Yes,' Rocco confirmed, telling her coolly, 'If you and I were to marry, then there would be no question of anyone trying to take Josh from you.'

'What? That's…that's not possible.'

Rocco frowned, his resolution, like his pride, hardened by her rejection and denial.

'Why not?'

You don't love me. How easily those words might have slipped from her lips—and how illuminatingly, shining an unwanted and far too bright light into the most private recesses of her own heart.

'It doesn't make sense,' Julie told him weakly.

'On the contrary—it makes perfect sense.' Rocco overruled her. 'I know what the lack of parental love and the loss of a mother can do to a child, and since it is within my power to ensure that that does not happen to Josh, then—'

'But to marry me? Josh is not your responsibility after all.'

'I cannot agree with that. Whilst you and Josh are living beneath my roof you are both as much my responsibility as my father's people are his. That is what it means to be a Leopardi. I cannot abdicate that responsibility any more than I can deny my name and my blood. It is my duty to honour my responsibility to my blood and to you.'

'That's…that's feudal—' Julie began, only to have Rocco stop her.

'You believe, do you not, that you have a responsibility towards Josh, and that you must put his needs first and above your own and do what is right for him?' he said.

Julie nodded her head, her heart sinking as she realised where this conversation might be leading.

'Then you must understand that I too have my own sense of responsibility.'

He meant what he was saying, Julie recognized, but she still shook her head and said, 'But we are nothing to you…'

'You are here beneath my roof. Therefore you are my responsibility,' Rocco repeated, before continuing. 'On the other hand, if I have misunderstood your feelings and you do not feel you have to put your nephew's best interests first—'

'Of course I do.'

'Then you will agree that in marrying me you will be doing exactly that and providing him not just with the security of two parents but also with financial security.'

What could she say? It was impossible to deny the logic of Rocco's argument.

Every word he said reinforced for Julie what she had already come to know about him— namely that he was a man whose sense of responsibility was incredibly deep.

Her emotions see-sawed wildly between hope and dread, longing and revulsion, need and pride. Rocco was offering her a way to secure Josh's future. But it was a permanent place in his heart that she longed and ached for, and that was never going to be on offer. Did she really want to submit herself to the emotional anguish of living with Rocco as his wife when he did not love her? Wouldn't it be better for her own safety to reject his proposal? But what about Josh? Wasn't it her duty to put his needs first? Hadn't she been worrying about raising Josh on her own, all too aware of how important it was going to be for Josh to have the right kind of man in his life to model himself on? Josh had no male relatives of his own blood; he only had her. If she married Rocco he would not only provide Josh with material security, he would also be there for him as a father. No matter what her own personal feelings, didn't she owe it to Josh to recognise how important a role Rocco could play in his life?

As though he had picked up on her own thoughts, Rocco continued firmly, 'It is Josh we must both think of first here. He is a child who has already lost his parents and his grandparents. He loves you and depends on you. You have said yourself that this woman who wishes to claim him is not a fit mother for him.'

'But marriage…' Julie protested weakly.

Rocco shrugged. 'You may think of it as a temporary business arrangement, if you wish.'

A business arrangement. How those words hurt her. But it was not her own feelings that mattered here, Julie reminded herself sternly.

'As Josh's stepfather I shall do everything within my power to ensure that he is happy and well cared for. And before you ask, no, I do not have any particular desire for children of my own. I am not my father's eldest son, after all, with a duty to provide an heir.'

And of course any marriage to her would not stop him from finding whatever sexual pleasure he wanted outside that marriage. Pain ripped through her, tearing away the pitiful attempt she had made to conceal her real feelings about him. She wanted to be the only woman he sought for pleasure; she wanted to be totally and completely his; she wanted his desire and his love.

Julie could taste the sour bitterness of her awareness of the bleakness of her future. But if she refused Rocco's proposal, and James's sister did try to get custody of Josh, how was she going to feel? She did not have the money to fight a lengthy court case, and neither did she have the emotional and physical reserves to cope with months and maybe years of not knowing whether she would have to give Josh up. She couldn't ignore the effect that kind of pressure was likely to have on Josh. And then there were the final implications of her solicitor's message...

Why was she hesitating? Logically, what Rocco was proposing was the ideal solution—

and if she wasn't careful he might start probing to find out why she was holding back, what personal emotions she might be hiding.

The thought of her humiliation were he to discover that she had fallen in love with him galvanised her into saying unsteadily, 'Marriage just seems such a big step to take.'

'Too big? And yet you have told me over and over again how committed you are to Josh—and were to the man who fathered him. He can never share your life, but Josh can.'

'I understand what you're saying, and I'm grateful to you for suggesting it,' Julie felt bound to say. 'But…well, it seems so huge…I mean, for you to marry me to protect Josh. You are being very generous to…to both of us, but I have my pride too, and the thought of taking advantage of your generosity worries me.'

'Does it? Or is it in reality the thought of me taking advantage of our marital status that is actually worrying you?' Rocco asked her silkily.

Immediately Julie's face flamed with guilt and longing.

'That never crossed my mind,' she protested untruthfully. Such a scenario had indeed crossed her mind, but she was afraid not of any advances on his part, but of her own reactions to him, and what they would betray. She could hardly admit that, though, could she?

'We have no time to lose,' Rocco told her, dropping the subject of her fears, much to her relief. 'The sooner we are married the sooner Josh will be safe. Then you can reply to your solicitor that there is no question of you giving Josh up, since your circumstances have changed and you are no longer a single mother but have a husband. But of course the decision must be yours.'

Helplessly, Julie admitted to herself that there was only one decision she could make.

She nodded her head, and told him huskily, 'Yes. I mean, yes—thank you. I would like to marry you.'

When Rocco had said that things needed to be done swiftly, that was exactly what he'd meant, Julie recognised two days later, her head spinning at the speed with which events were progressing.

Naturally as a Leopardi Rocco knew all the right people to talk to both in Sicily and in

London in order to make sure that the practical legalities were dealt with, but Julie was still astounded to learn that they were to be married the next morning in the small private chapel attached to the villa.

All the paperwork in preparation for their marriage had been completed, and once dinner was over Julie excused herself. The events of the last few days had exhausted her—if anything, even more emotionally than physically. Her medication was helping her to overcome her anaemia, but Julie doubted that the doctor would have anything to prescribe for the heartache that she suspected lay ahead of her.

She had brought Josh downstairs and put him in his buggy whilst they were having dinner, because Maria had gone to see her family and Julie hadn't wanted to leave Josh on his own in his bedroom.

Now, as she excused herself, Rocco got up to pull out her chair for her, saying something in Italian to his lawyer, who had joined them for dinner, before turning to her and stating firmly, 'I shall see you both to your room.' He wheeled the buggy towards the door.

Josh woke up when Rocco lifted him out of the buggy, and the look of recognition in her nephew's eyes, and the happy smile that followed it as he looked up at Rocco, were all the proof that Julie needed that she had made the right decision for Josh.

The right decision for Josh, but what about for her?

She was marrying a man who aroused her sexually and with whom she had fallen passionately in love—a man whose conversation stimulated her and whose personality intrigued her and challenged her. A man with whom she would never be bored and within whom she suspected there was a strong streak of compassion for others that with the right kind of encouragement could be harnessed to do so much good for others less happily circumstanced. There was nothing she wanted more than to be the true partner of such a man, to be loved by him as his one true soul mate. But that, of course, was a foolish fantasy.

They had reached her bedroom. Rocco opened the door for her and stepped back so that she could precede him into the room.

Three cream full-length dress bags had been placed on her bed.

'Wedding gowns,' Rocco told her. 'Unfortunately there isn't time for you to choose your own, so I arranged for a fashion house in Milan to send these out with Ricardo.'

Ricardo was the lawyer, and Julie wondered how he had felt about escorting three wedding gowns from Milan to Sicily.

Josh had gone back to sleep, so Rocco put him down in the middle of the bed, and then reached into his pocket, producing a small turquoise jeweller's box.

Mutely, Julie watched as he came towards her. There was a horrible hard lump of misery in her throat, and an aching sense of loss and despair in her heart.

No doubt the ring she was about to receive would be as tasteful and expensive as the wedding gowns lying on the bed. And just as devoid of any of the real feelings they should have signified as their marriage itself would be.

Rocco had flipped open the lid of the box, and just as she had guessed the glittering dazzle from the rings inside it made her blink.

The solitaire diamond surrounded by a circle of smaller diamonds and set on a diamond and white gold band perfectly matched the diamond and white gold wedding ring that went with it. They were rings that caught at the heart with their beauty and exclusively expensive allure, but diamonds were a poor substitute for love, Julie thought painfully.

Somehow she wasn't surprised that the rings should be so very much to her taste—nor that the engagement ring which Rocco insisted on sliding onto her finger fitted it perfectly.

He was still holding her hand. Without thinking Julie looked up at him, her eyes widening slightly in a mixture of panic and longing as she saw the way he was looking back at her, his eyes darkening as he shifted his gaze from her eyes to her mouth and then began to lower his head. His intention of kissing her was quite plain.

Ridiculously, Julie panicked, shaking her head and pulling back from him as she told him quickly, 'There's no need for that. We both know that it doesn't mean anything.'

Why was he frowning at her? She would have

thought that he'd be pleased that she was being so sensible and businesslike, that she was not expecting him to behave as though he was a real bridegroom-to-be and she his bride. If that had been the case then…

Then what? Then right now she would be in his arms, her love for him spilling emotionally from her heart as she told him how much his love meant to her?

A small noise indicated that Josh had woken up, and, glad of the opportunity to do so, Julie turned away from Rocco to go to her nephew.

Having picked Josh up, it was safe to turn round and look at him. She was holding Josh like a barrier between them.

There was something she had to say to him. She took a deep breath, and said huskily, 'Thank you.' She swallowed, and then added, 'For…for everything. I know this can't be something that you really want. It's different for me, of course. I have to put Josh first. But…what I'm trying to say is…I'm very grateful to you for what you're doing.'

Rocco nodded his head, but the grim look he was giving her suggested that her gratitude didn't really mean very much to him. Was he having second thoughts? Wishing that he hadn't behaved so gallantly and taken on such a heavy responsibility?

When he left without saying anything more, Julie didn't know whether to be relieved or disappointed.

In the corridor outside Julie's room, Rocco stared unseeingly into the shadows. His reaction when Julie had recoiled from him as he'd bent his head to kiss her had stunned him, catching him off guard. But it was irritation he felt, nothing else. Irritation because she was clinging so naïvely and stubbornly to her adolescent crush, elevating it to a status it didn't deserve. She had rejected his kiss out of some misguided loyalty to a man who had never taken the time to show her pleasure. Well, let her deny herself the pleasure they could have shared if she wished. Why should he care?

But he did care, Rocco recognised as he headed for the stairs. He cared very much. Abruptly he stopped in mid-step. He cared? For her? Was that his real motivation for marrying her? No! He was marrying her because it was his responsibility to do so and for no other reason.

* * *

Daylight was creeping into the room through the uncurtained windows as the night's shadows lifted. Julie didn't know whether to be alarmed or relieved. She had barely slept—how could she, knowing what the morning would bring?— and now that the day was here she could feel the enormity of what lay ahead flooding her senses.

Removed from their protective covers, the gowns fluttered like fragile ghosts in the breeze from the open windows. Julie had already made up her mind which one she would wear—the simplest of the three, in matt cream silk satin and cut on the bias, its seams sewn with tiny pearls. Pearls for tears? No, she mustn't think of that. It had a high neckline and long sleeves, and a small bustle at the back, falling into a demi-train. She had chosen it because she felt that its plainness and its high neckline and long sleeves were more suited to the occasion than the more flamboyant styles of the other two gowns.

There was no time for her to linger over her preparations.

Maria, who had brought her the breakfast she had not been able to eat, had returned to help her dress and take charge of Josh for her.

Julie leaned over the cot to look at the sleeping

baby. She could see for herself the way in which their time here had already benefited him. He looked so much healthier, and he was happier too. It had startled her at first to see the way Josh looked towards Rocco whenever he was in the same room. His delight when Rocco smiled at him or picked him up was plain to see. If he were never to see Rocco again he would miss him, but he was barely two months old—he would forget him.

It was all very well her telling herself that it would be wrong to deprive Josh of Rocco's presence in his life, but wasn't she only doing so to mask the fact that she wanted to marry Rocco? Rocco was not connected by blood in any way to Josh, after all. But that did not mean they could not form a deep emotional bond. Just as it had surprised her to see how Josh responded to Rocco, so too it had amazed her to see the genuine warmth and tenderness in Rocco whenever he was with Josh. Was she doing the right thing? Or was she rushing into something that she would later regret?

It was too late. Maria was holding out her dress for her.

Giving Josh a light kiss, Julie went back to

stand submissive whilst Maria fussed round her, her manner and her expression filled with the delight and excitement that Julie knew she should be sharing.

It felt so unreal, stepping into her wedding dress. In the past when she had dreamed of this moment she had imagined herself in her childhood home with her parents—not here, in this feudal land of powerful, arrogant men who lived by their word, their honour and their pride. She had dreamed of marrying James and of a quiet, steadfast love. Not Rocco and the fierce, dangerous passion he aroused in her.

Maria was sobbing emotionally, praising the beauty of her gown and her good luck in securing such a wonderful man—a Leopardi— for her husband.

All too soon it was time for her to go downstairs to where Rocco's lawyer was waiting to escort her to the private chapel. He told her Rocco was already waiting for her.

The chapel was small but magnificent, its ceiling and walls brilliantly frescoed with biblical images and its pews beautifully carved. Julie could feel the weight of its years of devotion, and panic started to fill her at the thought of the awesome nature of the commitment she was about to make here in this holy place.

She hesitated in mid-step and felt the quick look the lawyer gave her. She was doing this for Josh, Julie reminded herself shakily, and she focused on Rocco's ramrod-straight back. Somehow just looking at him calmed her, and filled her with a deep spiritual awareness of the purpose of the commitment she and Rocco were making, so that her body stopped trembling. The lawyer, who was holding her arm, paused to give her an approving smile, as though he sensed her determination to do what she felt so deeply to be right.

But it was only when Rocco turned to look at her that she felt truly able to take the final steps that brought her level with him, as though somehow he himself was drawing her to him and giving her strength.

The service was simple, its words timeless and beautiful and the priest compassionate and yet stern as he underlined the gravity of the commitment they were making, joining their hands and commanding them to repeat after him their vows to one another.

This time she did not evade Rocco's kiss. In fact she desperately wanted to cling to it and to him, needing reality in a world that seemed all too unreal.

In the small room off the chapel there were papers to sign, and then Rocco was guiding her back into the chapel and down the aisle to the font, where Maria and Josh, awake and dressed and lying happily in his buggy, were waiting for them.

It was done. Josh was safe. But at what cost to her? Only time would tell if she had the strength to endure her love for Rocco and his lack of love for her. It wasn't as though she hadn't already had practice, she reminded herself, remembering James. But her feelings for James couldn't in any way compare with what she felt for Rocco.

Rocco looked at Julie's pale, set face. She was his now. His wife. A feeling he couldn't analyse seized him: primitive, male, and very possessive. The satin gown caressed her body so lovingly that he almost felt jealous of its intimate contact with her, wanting to replace its touch with his own. He could see the admiring looks his lawyer was giving her, and he wanted to draw her away from him, to keep her from the desiring

looks of all other men and for himself alone. She
and the child were both now beneath his protection. His. He was now a husband and a father,
and his duty was to keep them both safe. Their
future was his responsibility.

A husband, but not a lover—nor loved.

Did he want to be?

That he should even need to ask himself that
question was a warning that rubbed against
Rocco's pride like wet sandpaper against tender
flesh.

It astonished Julie just how much attention to
detail Rocco had given to the outward form of
their marriage—there was a photographer to
capture their images, and a small, hastily
arranged but nonetheless elegant champagne reception to which a variety of local dignities had
been invited. Rocco informed Julie, as they stood
side by side whilst Rocco introduced her to their
guests, that it was expected and would give rise
to comment if he did not show public pride in
their marriage and in her as his wife.

'Oh, and by the way,' he added, 'I've told
Maria that rather than disrupt Josh, since his

nursery is off your bedroom, it makes sense for you to continue to sleep in your own room rather than move into the master bedroom.'

Simple enough words, and there had been a time when she would have received them with gratitude, but now they felt like a mortal blow to her heart, Julie admitted.

'I wouldn't want things any other way,' she managed to answer, but she didn't dare risk looking at him as she spoke, just in case he could see her real feelings in her eyes.

But what else could she reasonably have expected? She knew he didn't love her, that he had only married her for Josh's sake, and logically she ought to be pleased he had found such a tactful way of pointing out to her that he didn't want her sharing his bed, given his almost arrogantly alpha maleness.

Their 'guests' had left, Rocco was escorting his lawyer to a car waiting to take him to the private plane that would fly him back to the mainland, and Josh, who had been awake to be admired during the champagne breakfast, was now a soft, sleeping weight in her arms. The silk satin dress, for all its elegance, somehow felt tawdry, given the real reason for her marriage, and Julie longed to take it off and put on clothes that she had bought for herself, no matter how cheap and unstylish they might be compared with the things Rocco had bought for her. Like the champagne that had soured her palette and left her longing for clean, fresh water, those designer clothes were part of a lifestyle that was not really hers, and they reinforced the fact that she had in one sense been bought by Rocco just as easily as Antonio had bought her sister.

But for very different reasons. Everything she had agreed to and had done was for Josh's sake.

That wasn't true. Hadn't at least part of the reason she had agreed to marry Rocco been the fact that she had fallen in love with him, and had snatched eagerly at the opportunity to share his life?

Share his life? She was indeed a fool if she really thought there was any chance of that. If Rocco wouldn't let her share his bed then there was precious little hope that he would allow her to share anything else, was there? A single tear splashed down onto Josh's face, causing him to open his eyes and then yawn sleepily before closing them again. His trust in her touched Julie's heart, and she curved her mouth in a softly tender smile as she bent to wipe away the tear.

Watching her unobserved from the doorway, Rocco frowned. There could be only one reason for a bride to cry tears of sorrow on her wedding day, and that was because she had married the wrong man, her love having been given to someone else. Anyone observing her with Josh could see how much he meant to her—the child of the man she loved.

With the curves of her body hidden by the sleeping baby she looked more like a Madonna than a bride, untouchable and aloof. But he wanted to touch her, he wanted to hold her, he wanted to hear her cry out to him in her need as she had done before. He wanted her, Rocco admitted, stepping back from the doorway before Julie could see him mooning over her like some yearning lovesick adolescent. For a moment he wondered if that was why he had deliberately left it too late for his brothers to make it in time for the wedding.

No, he had done his duty by Julie and Josh, that was all. Now he had a duty to his business, to the construction site where he had had to postpone several important meetings in order to make time for today's hurried marriage.

There was no need for him to hang around the villa as though he was waiting around to beg for what few sparc crumbs of attention Julie might throw his way. He had better things to do with his time.

It was Maria who informed Julie that Rocco had gone out and that she didn't know when he would be back.

Was that sympathy or pity she could see in Maria's eyes? Julie wondered as she asked Maria to help her unfasten her wedding dress—a duty and a pleasure that should surely have been Rocco's. Only there was no pleasure for him in touching her, was there? Not for him. But for her that pleasure was the sweetest and the most dangerous she had ever known or would ever know.

CHAPTER TWELVE

IT WAS gone ten o'clock in the evening and
Rocco had still not returned. There was nothing
to keep her downstairs. The last thing she wanted
was for Rocco to come in and find her hanging
around as though she was waiting for him, desperate for his company. Maria had already
locked up, and she might as well go up to her
room as stay downstairs Julie acknowledged.

In the nursery Josh lay fast asleep, his eyelashes
fanning across his healthily pink cheeks. For his
sake if not for her own she knew beyond any
doubt that she had done the right thing. She had
no idea just why James's sister had decided that
she wanted Josh, but what Julie did know was that
she would never have been a good mother to him.

Her wedding dress had been carefully packed
away in its dress bag, and there was no sign
anywhere in the room that today had been her

wedding day unless it was in the new shine of her rings. There was certainly no husband—no Rocco here with her, to make the vows they had exchanged real in the only way a marriage could be made real.

Julie undressed and headed for the shower before changing her mind, tempted instead by the thought of a luxurious soak in the large deep bath.

Pinning up her hair, she started to run the bath. On impulse she closed the nursery door so that she wouldn't disturb Josh and switched on the bathroom's state-of-the-art music system, which was loaded with a wide selection of different kinds of music.

Tonight the haunting sound of female blues singers crooning about their lost love best suited her mood.

The bathroom was its own private oasis of blissful self-indulgence, and the music and the bittersweet scent of the bath oil she had chosen perfectly matched her mood of melancholy and longing. The blues music whispered its knowledge of what it meant to be a woman hungering for a man who did not hunger back for her.

The bath was deep enough for her to slide her

body beneath the water and let it lap at her throat, caressing her like warm scented silk. Her flesh was so aware of the pleasure it had known with Rocco and was now denied that every small movement of the water was almost a physical touch. If she closed her eyes it would be so easy to remember, to imagine, to transfer her memories of Rocco's possession from the past to the present, to pretend that she was in truth his bride, lying here waiting for him and for his caress…

Rocco heard the muted strains of music the minute he opened the door and walked into the bedroom. He had spent longer at the site than he had planned, and even though he'd known that Julie wouldn't have waited up for him there had been something about entering the darkened villa on this, his wedding night, that had touched a newly exposed nerve deep within his sense of self, where he felt most vulnerable. He had thought himself safe from the pain that came from emotional loss through the death of his mother, as though the intensity of that had seared and sealed away his vulnerability, but now he recognised that he had been wrong. Rocco didn't

like being wrong—about anything—and he liked
even less the driving need that had brought him
here to this night-shadowed bedroom that
smelled of the rose scent Julie had worn when
they exchanged their vows.

The bedroom was empty, and when he opened
the door to the nursery Josh, its only occupant,
lay sleeping peacefully in his cot. Closing the
nursery door as he exited, Rocco looked towards
the bathroom. A blues singer was sobbing out her
tale of angry, passionate grief, her song drowning
out the sound of his entrance. Julie was lying in
the bath, her eyes closed, damp tendrils of hair
escaping from her topknot to cling to her face.
She was lost, oblivious to his presence, her
parted lips and accelerated breathing telling his
senses that she had given herself over to some
private, sensual daydream. But not of him! Her
left hand rested on the side of the bath, devoid
of the ring he had placed there earlier.

A feeling Rocco didn't want to analyse ripped
through him in a tidal wave, sucking away reason
and replacing it with the powerful rip curl of
emotions it had dredged up from deep within him.

Julie was his wife, and this was their wedding

night. No way was he going to have her fanta-
sising about some other man. Without stopping
to analyse his own reactions, he strode over to
the bath, reaching down to take hold of her hand.

Julie opened her eyes and struggled to sit up,
shocked into a panicky reaction by the unexpect-
edness of Rocco's touch. The violence of her
movements sent the bathwater splashing over the
side of the bath, soaking Rocco's shirt and jeans.

'Where is your wedding ring? Why have you
taken it off?'

Why was he looking at her as though she had
committed some heinous crime? 'It's a bit loose
and I didn't want to lose it.'

'Liar. You took it off because you didn't want
to be reminded of me whilst you lay there imagining your precious James pleasuring you.'

They stared at one another, as though neither
of them could quite believe what Rocco had said.

'That's not true,' Julie denied.

'Isn't it? I'm not a fool. It was obvious when I
came in here where your thoughts were—as
obvious as the sensuality of their nature. Your
body can't lie about that even if you want to do so.'

Before she could stop him Rocco had drawn

his fingertip swiftly down her wet skin to the curve of her breast, unintentionally exposed when she had sat up in surprise. He moved along it to the flushed peak of her nipple, eagerly flaunting its erotic arousal.

'*Now* tell me that you weren't thinking about your lover,' Rocco challenged her angrily.

Julie tilted her chin. Her heart was thudding—with anger, she assured herself, even though she knew perfectly well that those jerky, fast-paced unsteady thuds within her ribcage were born more of excitement than anger, and that the sharp thrill of sensation shooting through her was pure, desire-driven heat.

'Very well, then,' she told him dangerously. 'Yes, I was thinking about my lover.' It was true, after all, even if he had mistaken the identity of that lover, not realising that it was Rocco himself she had been longing for and not James. 'And why shouldn't I if I want to?'

Now she really had shocked herself. And yet there was a thrilling sense of wanton delight in having said those words.

'Why shouldn't you?' Rocco's lips thinned, his eyes almost black as he stared down at her. 'Do you really need to ask me that? It's less than twenty-four hours since I took you as my wife.'

Fiery, illicit pleasure poured through her at the sound of those words, reinforcing for her everything she already knew about her own feelings.

She wasn't really actually trying to egg Rocco on to physically possess her, was she? And if she was? He was her husband, after all, so she had the right…

The right? To what? To torment a man into making love to her when he didn't really want to? Hot shame burned her conscience.

'I think you should leave,' she told Rocco unsteadily. The bathwater had gone cold and she was starting to shiver, chilled as much by her self-disgust as the cooling water.

'Really?'

Rocco's voice was as soft as silk, wrapped around the wicked danger of a sharp stiletto blade—like whispers from the shadows that held a Pandora's box of enticing delight laced with unknown dangers.

'Well, I think I should do this.'

His iron grip already held her shackled, but it was her own desire for him that really held her imprisoned and was her greatest enemy, Julie recognised as he lifted her from the bath with one easy movement that barely moved his chest, ignoring the water cascading from her as easily as he ignored her feebly voiced protests. In the background the music rose to a crescendo of pleading, but Julie no longer needed to plead for her lover.

'Your clothes are wet.' What an inane comment to make.

'Then, like a good wife, you'd better take them off for me.' Rocco mocked her.

Undress him? Julie felt boneless with the melting heat of her own longing.

The signs of her desire were clearly evident, but that desire was not for him, Rocco warned himself. Her thoughts had been with another man when she had lain there beneath the water, thinking of his touch.

He wanted her. He was her husband.

He took her hands and placed them on the wet fabric that covered his chest. 'Undress me,' he commanded.

If she did as he was demanding she would be lost.

'No,' she refused, shaking her head. 'I don't want to.'

It was a lie, but he couldn't know that. For a minute, when he released her hands, she thought he was going to let her go and walk away. But then he cupped her face and started to kiss her—oh, so slowly and deliberately—in such an intensely focused way that she knew exactly what the punishment for refusing him was going to be.

She tried to resist, keeping her lips tightly locked together, keeping her eyes wide open and refusing to look at him, tensing her whole body against his slow, sensual seduction of her.

It had to be someone else who was making that small husky sound of pleasure. Another Julie who was tipping back her head and closing her eyes as she willingly offered herself up for his caress, who trembled wildly in a paroxysm of fevered arousal when his fingertips gently brushed her throat and then her breasts, whilst his mouth coaxed and tormented her own into eager participation in the kind of kiss that ravished her senses and laid bare her longing for him.

She wanted him so badly. She wanted him body to body with her, flesh to flesh, touch to touch. Her hunger for him was fed by the thrust of his tongue against her own and the touch of his hands on her naked body, caressing her naked breasts, shaping the indentation of her waist and the curve of her hip. His fingers dipped into her own secret wetness, sending showers of fireworks of liquid pleasure exploding through her.

She had to touch him as he was touching her. Impatiently she started to tug buttons through buttonholes in the urgency of her need, meeting and matching the passion of his kisses as the sensation of his skin beneath her fingertips accelerated her arousal.

Her lips followed the eager, explorative journey of her fingertips, tracing the strong column of his throat and the broad sweep of his chest. His body hair was soft against her mouth; her fingers were clumsy on the belt that barred her way to the intimacy she longed for.

Her protest when Rocco suddenly seized her hands to stay them was a raw sound of female deprivation.

'Hush. Wait,' Rocco told her, sweeping her up in his arms to carry her from the bathroom into the bedroom, where he placed her on the large bed.

Looking up at him through the shadows, Julie felt as though her heart was so filled with love for him that it couldn't contain the intensity of her emotions, that it was spilling from her like tears of acute pleasure. She lifted her hand to his face, tracing its shape wonderingly. If he left her now— But he was removing the rest of his clothes, and her heart lifted on the surging tide of her own desire as she looked at him, visually absorbing and recording every precious detail of his physical presence before finally giving in to her need to reach out and stroke her fingertips along the hard, erect length of him.

Her intimate touch tipped Rocco over the edge of his self-control. He took hold of her, kissing her mouth and then her breasts, tugging gently on her nipples, and then less gently when he felt the immediate surge of her response and heard her cry out to him. Her hands reached down to hold his head against her body. His hands found her and caressed her, pleasured her to the point where her pleasure was almost more than she could endure.

'My love,' Julie whispered emotionally, moving feverishly against his touch, commanded by it and yet driven to push past that command to a place where she could command him. 'My only love.'

Thought and feeling melded together, burning away the old Julie, setting their mark on her for ever. She didn't even see the look of dark bitterness shadowing Rocco's eyes as he listened to her, much less register the moment of tension in his body as he swung between pride and desire, wanting her so desperately and yet filled with a need to reject that wanting, having heard her proclaim her love for another man.

In the end his desire won. The pleasure his touch gave her was his mark of possession as he waited for her to come down from that place where he had taken her with the knowing stroke of his fingers to the plateau where his own desire waited impatiently for her.

How well they fitted together—as though she had been made only for him, Julie thought dizzily as he stroked into her, filling her, re-sensitising her still-responsive flesh. Her muscles closed possessively around him, wanting him, rocking with sweet erotic pleasure at each movement within her, until the sweetness was stripped away and there was only a dark, raw passion that had her clinging to him as they swung above the chasm. She cried out to him in the darkness, feeling him sweep them both upwards to brilliance so surely that she was both laughing and crying with joy when he held her through the powerful spasms of their shared orgasm.

It was over. She felt so weak, so lost—and so afraid. Rocco was lying on his back, apart from her instead of holding her as she longed for him to do.

She had called him her love, but of course he was no such thing, Rocco acknowledged. She had meant those words for another man; the man she had exchanged inside her head for him.

What a fool he had been not to recognise until he had her exactly what had happened to him. He didn't just want her. He loved her.

Rocco was regretting what had happened. Julie could tell. That was why he was lying so far away from her. How was it possible to have known so much happiness and yet now feel such dreadful pain? She longed for him to hold her and to whisper to her that he wanted her love. What a fool she was.

CHAPTER THIRTEEN

THEY had been married ten days. Maria had informed her again that Rocco had left the villa early to attend a site meeting. Every night Rocco came to her bed and made love to her, and every morning she woke up alone. Painful though it was for her to admit it, Julie acknowledged that she couldn't avoid knowing that the physical intimacy they now shared had, instead of bringing them closer together, actually destroyed the bond she had felt they were beginning to build. Rocco no longer sought her out to talk with her. He no longer smiled at her, or seemed to want to be with her, and even in bed there was a repressed tension about him that was almost tinged with anger—because he regretted his generosity in marrying her?

It was Julie's nature to give generously to those she loved, without counting the cost to herself, and never more so than when it came to Rocco. She hated the thought that she could be blighting his life and shadowing his enjoyment of it. She wanted him to be happy, to see him smile, hear him laugh. But even if that meant it was someone else, another woman, whose presence gave him those things?

She loved him, and that meant putting his happiness first, Julie insisted to herself as she reached out to unclamp Josh's too exploratory fingers from the edge of the rug on which he was lying, which he was now trying desperately to tug from beneath himself.

The patio where Julie was sitting was warm from the morning sun; her body still had that lethargic ache that came from intense sexual pleasure. Julie looked up lazily when Maria suddenly appeared, her laziness disappearing when Maria told her importantly, 'Il Principe is here to see you.'

The Prince? Rocco's father? She had understood from Rocco that his father was suffering from a terminal heart condition and was virtually bedridden. Why on earth would he want to see *her*?

'Are you sure it is me he wishes to see and not Rocco?' she asked Maria uncertainly.

'It is you he wishes to see,' Maria confirmed, adding, 'Quick—you must hurry and not keep him waiting.'

Against her better judgement Julie found that she was allowing herself to be coaxed and bullied into hurrying back into the house, Josh clasped tightly in her arms.

Maria had shown Rocco's father into the grandest of all the formal salons, twenty metres long and fifteen metres wide, with heavy rococo décor and gilded furniture. Its rich blue embroidered silk drapes threw shadows that reached out to create dim pools of darkness, making it almost impossible to see anything clearly.

It was a shock to see Rocco's good looks stamped so clearly on the face of the man seated in a wheelchair behind which was standing a harassed-looking middle-aged man, whom Julie assumed must be his attendant. The Prince's mouth was etched with pride, and his eyes were colder than polished black marble.

He was, Julie recognised, everything that Rocco had warned her he would be, and her heart ached for the three small boys left to this man's pitiless care by the death of the mother who had loved them.

'So!' His angry gaze raked Julie from top to toe. 'There is no need for me to ask why you married my son. There can only be one reason.'

Rocco, alerted to his father's arrival at the villa by a phone call from Maria, arrived just as his father and Julie were confronting one another. Both of them were oblivious to his presence, the hostility between them so powerful it was almost like a force field.

'Actually, there are two reasons,' Julie corrected the Prince determinedly. 'One is my love for my nephew, and the other is my love for Rocco himself.'

Pride and truth rang in the clear enunciation of her words, causing Rocco to remain where he was instead of alerting them to his presence.

'You love my son?' Rocco's father gave a contemptuous shrug. 'Of course you do. After all, he is a rich man.'

'I love Rocco for what he is himself, not for his wealth. I would love him just as much if he was poor. In fact I wish he was,' Julie told the Prince passionately.

Rocco's father gave her another cold look.

'Such words are the words of the ignorant and the foolish. How naïve you are. I suppose you believe that Rocco returns your feelings, do you? Your kind always do.'

Rocco had heard enough. He wasn't about to let his father verbally abuse and hurt Julie. He started to move forward, but once again the sound of Julie's emotionally charged voice stopped him.

'No. I don't,' Julie answered her inquisitor. 'I know that Rocco married me for reasons of duty and of…of chivalry. Because he wants to protect Josh from being stolen from me to suffer as he himself did as a child.'

She could be accused of being cruel, Julie knew, but hadn't this man been cruel to his three eldest sons? Hadn't he denied them the love they had had every right to expect from him? Shouldn't she, out of her love for Rocco, redress the balance if only a little, and show him what an honourable and wonderful man his third son was—even if his father didn't have the wisdom to see it for himself?

'I don't love Rocco because he is your son, or because he has wealth and position. I love him because despite everything he has had to endure the love his mother bore him has touched his heart and made him something that money can never buy.'

'And what might that be?'

'Rocco may have his pride—the pride of his ancestors—but he also has magnanimity of spirit. He has compassion and wisdom; he understands the true meaning of love. He is a man who as a child never knew the true love of a father, and yet he has grown beyond that, instead of allowing it to cripple him emotionally, to take into his protection a child who has no claim whatsoever on him.

'You may be a Prince, but Rocco bears a higher and far more worthy title—and that is the title of a good and honest man, the best of men. The kind of man other men will always look up to because of what he is, not who he is, the kind of man who deserves to have a loving father who values him as he should be valued. I will never burden Rocco with my love. He already has enough to bear. But neither will I allow you to think that he needs anything to win a woman's love other than himself. I would be proud to follow him in rags to the end of the earth if he asked that of me.'

She almost threw her last words at Rocco's father, turning on her heel as she did so, unable to endure another second in his company. She was not going to allow Rocco's father to denigrate the man she loved, no matter how afraid he made her feel, Julie told herself fiercely—and then gasped with shock when she saw Rocco standing in front of her.

'Julie.'

He was angry with her. He had to be. Shaking her head, Julie evaded him, holding Josh tightly as she fled.

Rocco let her go. What he needed to say to her was best said in private—and besides, there were things he had to say to his father, issues that must now be dealt with.

Approaching the wheelchair, he stood looking down at the man seated in it. Falcon had taught him by example to give their father respect, as a matter of duty and as a gift of love and honour to their dead mother, but it was not a respect that came freely and lovingly from his heart, Rocco acknowledged.

'How could you, a Leopardi, marry this—this nobody?' the Prince demanded furiously. 'You are my son. You have a duty to me and to your name. Now you have shamed me and that name by marrying this *nothing*, who should have been sent back where she came from once you knew that her child was not Antonio's. It is no wonder that you married in secret to hide your shame.'

There was so much Rocco wanted to say to his father. But he could see where the swollen vein in his temple had started to throb and pulse under the force of his anger, and he could see, too, the anxious concern of the medical attendant Dr Vittorio had placed in charge of the Prince's day-to-day care.

How pitiful he was, this man who had dominated his childhood and who had filled Rocco with both the longing for approval and attention and the bitter realisation that he would never receive them.

Now, as a result of his treatment of them as children, at a time when a good father should at this stage of his life have commanded their love and care, his father could only command the cold emptiness of duty. Rocco thought of the way in which Josh was already recognising him, smiling up at him and holding out his arms to him. He made himself a promise that the baby's trust would never be abused, and that the small shoot of love was something he would protect and nurture for as long as Josh needed those things from him.

'What you mistake for secrecy, Father, was in fact speed. And the reason I married Julie with speed was because I was afraid she might realise how unworthy of her I am and that I would lose her.'

As he spoke Rocco recognised that there was a great deal of truth in what he was saying.

'Far from being ashamed of my wife, I am very proud of her, and there is nothing I would have liked more than to have my brothers witness our marriage.'

'Your brothers! Bah! The three of you cling together, speaking with one voice, when it is to me, your father, that you owe your loyalty.'

'It is not loyalty that binds the three of us together, Father. It is our mutual love for one another. And as for our loyalty, there we have followed your example. Our loyalty is given to the Leopardi name, not those who carry it.'

Rocco watched as something that might have been vulnerability flickered across his father's face, quickly replaced by anger.

'With every word you say you show how much you are the son of your mother,' the Prince told Rocco with contempt. 'I came here to see what could be salvaged from the folly of this marriage, and was fully prepared to pay this Englishwoman to leave. But now I shall leave you to suffer the consequences of your own making.'

'As all men must,' Rocco agreed calmly, then ignored his father to speak to his attendant. 'My father treats you very unfairly, Aldo. I know it is through no fault of yours that Dr Vittorio's instructions have been ignored. If you will take my father back to the castle, I shall speak to Dr Vittorio and ask him to call there and see my father as soon as he can. Father, Aldo will take you home now.'

Rocco could see expressions of fury, bafflement and confusion crossing his father's face at Rocco's refusal to engage in an acrimonious exchange of words with him.

'I know you will be disappointed that it has not been possible to find this child Antonio said existed, but maybe it is for the best,' Rocco told his father, exhaling before acknowledging that Julie had already had a very profound effect upon him, even if she herself didn't know it. Why else, after all, would he be standing here like this, considering his father's feelings, and actually feeling pity for him where once he would have only felt bitterness and loathing.

'Aldo, take me back to the car,' the Prince ordered his attendant.

Silently Rocco walked alongside the wheelchair as he escorted his father out to his waiting car.

Before Aldo activated the electric ramp that would lift the chair into place in the specially adapted car, Rocco placed his hands on his father's shoulders and bent to kiss him, first on one cheek and then the other. Not as a supplicant, or even as a survivor, but for the first time as a victor who knew that his victory was unchallengable and who could afford to be generous because of that knowledge.

It was Julie who had given him that gift.

Julie.

As the car pulled away Rocco looked up towards the second-floor windows.

Maria was waiting for him in the hall.

'I have something I need to discuss with my wife,' he told her crisply. 'And I do not wish to be disturbed by anyone for any reason.'

When he crossed the hallway a second time he was carrying an ice bucket containing a bottle of champagne and two glasses.

Maria smiled happily to herself. A house like the villa needed a big family to fill it—many *bambini*—and, unless she was very wrong, the first of them wouldn't be very long in the creating. She must have a word with her daughter. She was just the right age to train up as a nursery nurse…

'I think there's something you need to tell me.'

How calm Rocco sounded as he carefully placed the champagne bucket down on a small table next to the bedroom armchair along with two glasses.

Julie felt sick with despair. She had known that he was bound to demand an explanation for what he had obviously overheard.

'I'm sorry if I spoke out of turn and…and offended your father.' Her voice was stiff with the need to protect herself, and she wasn't going to risk looking at him.

'To hell with my father. He isn't what matters right now. Neither is he what I'm talking about, and you know it.'

'No, I don't.'

She was almost stammering now, her heart hammering as she wondered wildly just how much Rocco might have overheard.

Rocco counted inwardly to ten. They could play this game all day long, but right now it was the end result he needed and wanted, not the playing of it. He turned his back on Julie, busying himself with opening the bottle of champagne and pouring two glasses, handing her one as he sought an eloquent way to seek an answer to the question that burned in his heart.

Finally he asked baldly, 'You told my father that you love me, but you told me that you still love James. Which is the truth?'

Dared she tell him? Dared she not? Julie took a quick gulp of her champagne, half gasping under the influence of the bubbles. Rocco was looking at her in the most extraordinary way, with the most wonderful expression in his eyes. As though…as though his gaze was somehow caressing and reassuring her—or was that simply the effect of the champagne? If so… Recklessly Julie took another deep gulp. Now she felt positively light-headed, free of all her doubts and her inhibitions, suddenly overwhelmingly proud of her love for him.

'The truth is…'

'The truth is…?' Rocco prompted.

Julie looked wildly towards the nursery door. This was one occasion on which she would actually be grateful if Josh did wake up without finishing his nap. But her nephew seemed to be more inclined to support his new father than her, because he remained soundly asleep.

'The truth?' Rocco repeated.

'I love you,' Julie told him shakily. 'I didn't mean to, and I certainly didn't want to, but I do.'

The champagne glass was removed from her hand with such speed that she barely had time to blink before she was in Rocco's arms and he was demanding against her lips, 'Tell me that again.'

She tried to frame the words, but how could she

when Rocco was licking and nibbling at her lips? He was teasing them with the stroke of his tongue, tormenting her to the point where the only sound she was capable of making was a long moan of hungry need followed by a soft sound of pleasure when Rocco answered the need and kissed her with all the passion and love she had so longed for.

Later, lying together naked in bed, their bodies sated and the air around them soft with the echo of their mutually given pledges of love for one anther, Julie traced the arrogant line of Rocco's jaw, laughing when he took hold of her hand and pressed a fiercely possessive kiss into her palm.

'There's still some champagne left,' he told her.

Julie laughed and went slightly pink. She had protested at first when he had poured some of the champagne onto her skin, kissing her and tasting her through it, but she hadn't protested for very long.

'If we have a daughter we are not going to call her Cristal,' Julie warned him.

Rocco grinned, the sensuality of the way he

was looking at her making her heart turn over with joy and love.

'If we have a daughter I shall no doubt feel compelled to lock any man who offers her champagne in my father's dungeons.'

'I thought we might name her after your mother.'

They looked at one another.

'You really think…just now…we…?' Rocco asked tenderly.

Julie nodded her head. 'Yes,' she told him simply. 'After the way you loved me, it just isn't possible that we haven't created a new life. It was so magical, Rocco, so powerful and wonderful, and I love you so very much.'

'You tugged on my heartstrings the first time I saw you, do you know that?'

'What? Looking like a drowned rat?'

'A drowned rat with the heart of a lioness and the spirit of a dove. My one and only love, my heart,' Rocco told her softly, and he took her in his arms and kissed her.